DATE DUE			

Summer Road Trip

Vegas

BY NICK DAY

EPIC Escape

An Imprint of EPIC Press
abdopublishing.com

Vegas
Summer Road Trip

Written by Nick Day

Copyright © 2018 by Abdo Consulting Group, Inc.

Published by EPIC Press™
PO Box 398166
Minneapolis, MN 55439

Cover design by Christina Doffing
Images for cover art obtained from iStock
Edited by Rue Moran

LIBRARY OF CONGRESS CATALOGING-IN-PUBLICATION DATA
Names: Day, Nick, author.
Title: Vegas/ by Nick Day
Description: Minneapolis, MN : EPIC Press, 2018 | Series: Summer road trip
Summary: After both getting rejected by their prom dates, two best friends, Mitch and Kendra,
    decide to leave their high school woes behind. What follows is a wild ride through roadside
    diners, the endless desert, the alluring Las Vegas Strip—and encounters with danger Mitch
    and Kendra hoped to never find.
Identifiers: LCCN 2016962619 | ISBN 9781680767278 (lib. bdg.)
    | ISBN 9781680767834 (ebook)
Subjects: LCSH: Adventure stories—Fiction. | Travel—Fiction. | Teenagers—Fiction.
    | Las Vegas Strip (Nev.)—Fiction | Young adult fiction.
Classification: DDC [FIC]—dc23
LC record available at http://lccn.loc.gov/2016962619

*To Ryan, Ben,
Dylan, Ella, and Brendan*

Chapter One

MITCH MATLIN HAD ALWAYS BEEN A ROMANTIC. At just four years old, he would beg his parents to let him re-watch, over and over again, their dusty VHS copy of *An Affair to Remember*. He had a *Breakfast at Tiffany's*-themed eighth birthday party. In his teenage years—when everyone is hiding something—Mitch was forced to keep his love for romance on the down-low. But now, in his senior year of high school, Mitch had finally found the perfect outlet for his lifelong obsession: prom.

It was a rainy, sticky May night in Salt Lake City, and Mitch was up late finalizing his plans. The next day—a Thursday, the day before prom tickets went on sale—he was going to absolutely *nail it*. East High had been buzzing for months about this year's prom. The theme was "A Night on the Las Vegas Strip," which would include poker tables, a big-band orchestra, and even more glamour on display than usual.

Mitch had been perfecting the plan his entire life, and now it would be put into motion. It was a plan so perfect, Mitch thought, that it would work on anyone—even Nora Dickinson, the class valedictorian, class president, and unanimous Homecoming Queen, four years in a row.

It didn't matter that he and Nora barely knew each other, Mitch consoled himself. The perfect ask—and this would be *textbook*—was universal.

The old-school '80s boom box sat at the end of Mitch's bed. Beside it sat a blank cassette tape he had just bought at Walgreens down the street. When he laid the tape down on the checkout counter, the cashier, a white-haired older woman, looked at him while smirking and said, "Even *I* don't remember how to use these things!"

Making a mixtape—not a mix-CD, not a Spotify playlist—was integral to the plan. But now, looking at the boom box and the tape, Mitch realized he had no idea how to make one.

"Come on, Matlin," Mitch muttered to himself. "You're gonna lose out on Nora because you can't figure out how to use a cassette tape? You're never gonna get anyone to love you unless you cure your bad case of Too-Millennial-to-Function disease." He rubbed his hands through his shaggy brown hair, coming close to pulling it all out in agony.

Rather than blindly trying things and risking breaking the stereo, Mitch picked up his phone and called the one person he knew could calm him down. After just one ring, a voice came up on the other end.

"'S'up?"

"Kendra!" Mitch exclaimed. His best friend for years, Kendra would listen and probably get him back on the right track. The whole issue of prom dates would have been much simpler if Kendra and Mitch had any romantic interest in each other, but that was never going to happen. After so many years of being friends, they treated each other like siblings. And siblings don't usually go to prom together. "Things are getting really desperate over here," Mitch said.

"What, you get caught in your zipper again?" she asked, laughing at her own joke.

"Spiritually, yes!" Mitch said. "I'm trying to make this effing mixtape for Nora."

"Whoa," Kendra said, sounding genuinely surprised. "Dude, this is so last-minute! I thought this was your Plan of a Lifetime."

"I know, I know," Mitch said. "I've been picking out songs for months, but I didn't realize actually *making it* would be so complicated. This thing I found online says I have to play the whole song *out loud* from the radio and record it to the tape while it's playing! That's gonna take hours!"

"Yeah, man," Kendra said. "Times were tough back in 1985."

"There's no other way to do it?"

"I don't think so," Kendra said. "I mean, the last time I made a mixtape was for my elementary school boyfriend. I kind of gave up after that. I think it was just 'She Will Be Loved' over and over again."

"Well, at least my song choice is better than that," Mitch said. "Want to hear what I picked?"

"Not really, bro," Kendra said. "I'm putting the finishing touches on my plan, too."

"You don't sound as stressed out as me," Mitch said. "I'm jealous."

"Well, I'm not going overboard like you," Kendra said. "I'm going for subtlety. I know that's what Adam wants. So, the flash mob is only gonna have forty people instead of a hundred. Seems good, right?"

Mitch could practically hear her winking on the other end. He smiled. Kendra was just as much of a hopeless romantic as he was. "I just can't get over that *you're* asking *him*," he said.

"Hey, join me in the twenty-first century, dude," Kendra said. Mitch could hear her smirking on the other end of the line. "Jenny Lewis asked Dante King two years ago. Do you remember who Dante King was?"

"Of course," Mitch said. Dante King was the captain of the basketball team that year—the team that had won East High's first state championship in the history of the school.

"Right," Kendra said. "And when he said yes, she officially changed the game. She was like the Susan B. Anthony of prom."

"I can't even believe how confident you are," Mitch said. "I've come close to scrapping the whole thing, like, eight times tonight."

"My plan is foolproof," Kendra said. "I mean . . . at least I actually sort of *know* the guy I'm asking." Mitch's stomach sank at Kendra's diss.

"I know," he said, sighing. "But, like, she knows who I *am,* right?" Kendra didn't answer right away. "Right?!" Mitch bellowed.

"Dude," Kendra said. "I don't know what that girl knows. I'm just . . . I'm a little nervous for you, man.

Why don't you ask someone you actually know? It wouldn't even be fun to go with Nora, she'd probably ditch you as soon as you got there!"

"But none of the girls I know see me like that," Mitch said. "You know it's true. Sure, there's Molly and Janelle and Julia and everybody, and of course I like them, but they've totally friend-zoned me! I'm trying to get a smooch at the end of the night, know what I mean?"

"I hear you, I hear you," Kendra said. "Right there with you."

"Go big or go home," Mitch said.

"For sure," said Kendra. "Leave it all on the court."

"Alright, I should go," Mitch said, looking back down at the boom box and the tape. "I have ninety minutes of my perfect playlist to listen to while hoping this big hunk of plastic actually still does something."

"Word," Kendra said. "*Hasta mañana.*"

– – –

Kendra tossed the phone down on her desk beside her computer. She was glad Mitch had a reason to hang up—she was working against the clock, too. Because unlike what she had told Mitch, things weren't exactly going according to plan.

Kendra's fingers flew over the keys of her MacBook as she responded to the endless Facebook messages rolling in. The flash mob she had planned for tomorrow, aimed at winning Adam Green's heart, was crumbling. Kendra had asked one hundred people to take part in it, knowing that some would cancel. But now more than seventy had cancelled on her, and the remaining thirty were on the brink.

"Ten people is not a flash mob," Kendra whispered to herself. "That's not even a flag football team."

On paper, the plan was genius. Who could say no to a performance by East High's award-winning music and theatre students? She made an a cappella arrangement of Adam's favorite song, "MMMBop" by Hanson—his parents' favorite band from the '90s—and choreographed an entire number. The mob was going to assemble right at the end of the school day, surrounding Adam and Kendra, and standing there, immersed in the music, Kendra would pop the question.

But now, looking at the messages popping up on her computer screen, Kendra was sweating bullets.

Hey girl, ugh my mom needs the car so I have to get home right after school tomorrow, sry!

Yo I didn't have time to learn the music, count me out

So sorry, I'm gonna be up late studying tn so I'll have to go right home and fall asleep lol ugh, I'm such a grandma!

And on and on.

Don't worry about the music! Kendra typed frantically. Just lip-sync, I'll play the song out of my Jambox!

She responded to another, from Maya Anderson, hoping she was still online to read it. I'll bring you a Red Bull! It'll just be five minutes, you don't even have to dance if you're tired, just stand there smiling!

Kendra untied her long jet-black hair from its ponytail and wound it all up in a topknot. She went to her bed and grabbed the small stuffed Jack the Jackal doll she'd had since before she could remember. Kendra got up early on Saturday mornings to watch Jack the Jackal cartoons from preschool to the end of middle school, when she forced herself to stop watching them, since it was kid stuff, and she was no longer a kid. She held the doll under her chin and nuzzled it, the only thing that never failed to make her feel better. "Oh, Jack," she cooed. "What am I gonna do?"

She had the increasing feeling that things were not going to turn around in her favor. *Of course it happens this way,* Kendra mused. *The two most romantic people at East High aren't interested in each other and can't get anybody else to pay attention.*

– – –

The next day flew by in one big blur. Kendra had a critique done on her charcoal drawings in art class; she could barely remember a word anybody said, positive or negative.

Suddenly, it was almost 3 p.m., game time. Kendra,

sitting in Calculus, played out the whole event in her head: the courtyard outside the main building, covered in dewy grass; the sun peeking through the low-hanging clouds; people milling about in every direction, headed to buses and cars—and then, bam!

Kendra ran through in her mind the list of twenty names she had talked back into participating. *Maybe,* she thought, *that's the perfect amount for Adam. He doesn't like being the center of attention anyway!*

Anticipating the end of class, the other students around her got up, packed their bags, and lingered near the door. Mr. Krulich, their crusty middle-aged teacher wearing a Utah Jazz T-shirt, turned around in his creaky desk chair. "Hey now," he said, "that's all fine, but don't go until—"

The bell rang, cutting him off, and the students bolted out the door. Kendra pushed forward through the mob, knowing that time was of the essence. She spotted Adam ahead of her, as planned. Kendra knew that Adam's seventh-period class was just across the hall. She pulled out her phone and texted the group thread with all the flash mob participants: It's go time! Courtyard in three minutes!

Her stomach churning, Kendra bustled on, keeping an eye on Adam. Then, appearing seemingly out of nowhere, came Mitch, walking in the opposite direction. He smiled at her as he spotted her, and held up his hand for a high five.

"Go get 'em, tiger," Mitch said.

"You, too," Kendra muttered nervously, giving him a tepid slap on the palm.

Hurrying down the main staircase towards the front door of the building, Kendra checked her phone again. No responses on the group thread. *Well,* Kendra said to herself, *that's probably no big deal. Everybody's leaving class. They know the plan. Why would they need to look at their phones?* She kept repeating this to herself as her feet pushed onward, seemingly of their own volition.

Suddenly, she was throwing open the front doors and walking into the courtyard. She immediately stopped short as cold, fine, misty rain settled over her head and face and started soaking into the fabric on her Keds. *My adorable, out-of-the-box fresh, baby-blue Keds!*

Umbrellas sprang up all around her, and people hurriedly walked to buses and cars. Kendra wanted to scream, *No! Wait! Just slow down!*

She kept an eye on Adam, watching him make his way across the courtyard. Adam was without an umbrella. Sensing her opportunity, Kendra bolted across the sodden grass toward him, slinging her backpack off her shoulders.

"Adam!" Kendra called brightly, coming up behind him. Adam stopped and turned to look over his shoulder and smiled upon seeing Kendra. His chestnut-brown eyes meeting hers made Kendra lose track of where she was and what she was doing, and she had to mentally slap herself to stay focused.

"Oh, hey!" Adam said. "Hey, I was gonna text you—do you want to get a group together to see the new *Avengers* movie this weekend?"

"Uh, sure, that sounds good . . . " Kendra started. The last thing she wanted to talk about right now was the stupid Avengers! Trying to stay on topic, Kendra looked for a grand gesture. "Here," Kendra grunted, hiking her own backpack up over Adam's head, only somewhat protecting him from the drizzle. Adam stood three inches taller than Kendra, and immediately she realized she did not have the muscle mass to keep this up for long.

"Oh," Adam said. "Thanks." He looked completely confused, as if he was looking at a new animal species no one had ever seen before.

"No problem," Kendra said, though her arms were already shaking. She cursed herself for bringing her AP Chemistry, Spanish, *and* English textbooks home for the night. Gritting her teeth into a smile, she said, "Wow, it sucks out here."

What?! "It sucks out here"? Kendra wanted to slap herself.

But Adam laughed. "Yeah, absolutely," he said. "And I was getting all excited for it to be a nice, pretty spring day."

"Yeah," Kendra managed.

"Well, I should keep walking," Adam said, putting one foot in front of the other.

"Oh yeah, me too," Kendra said. She started walking in exact time with Adam, still holding the twenty-pound backpack aloft.

"You really don't have to keep doing that," Adam said. Kendra frantically looked around the courtyard for everyone—anyone—who said they would do the flash mob. Where were they? Had *all* of her friends bailed on her? Really?

They were nearing the street, where Kendra knew that Adam would turn left and get on the number seven bus home. Realizing she was going to have to do all of this herself, Kendra pulled the backpack down, and leapt in front of Adam, blocking his way.

"Mmm-bop, dip a dop da ooh bop, ba doo-ee-oo ba, mmm-bop dip a dop da-ooo, yeah, yeah," she sang, trying desperately to remember the tune to the stupid Hanson song. Could Adam even tell what she was trying to do? Did he think she was just speaking in tongues?

Kendra smiled broadly, now wild-eyed with desperation. She spread her arms wide and forcefully step-touched side to side like a demented Madonna backup dancer.

"What . . . is happening?" Adam asked, slack-jawed. "Are you okay?"

Kendra stopped, breathing hard. She dropped her backpack on the sopping-wet grass. Her mouth dry and her arms trembling from overexertion, she looked up into Adam's eyes and forced a big smile.

"Prom?"

– – –

Across town, Mitch was close to hydroplaning on his Schwinn road bike as he flew towards his house. The rolling streets of his leafy neighborhood were slick with rain, but he refused to slow down. This afternoon was all in the timing, and if that meant skinning a knee, or running part of the way because his bike broke in half, so be it.

Skidding into his driveway, Mitch hopped off his bike and bolted into his house. Charging up the stairs, Mitch slipped off his backpack and chucked it on the floor just inside his room. Quickly, he pulled out his phone and checked his texts. There was one from his friend Danny. Since Danny lived across the street from the Dickinsons and went to a different school that let out earlier in the day, Mitch had charged him with sentry duty.

Still not home, bro, Danny had said. That message had come in ten minutes ago.

How bout now? Mitch texted, his thumbs trembling. Knowing he couldn't do anything without a green light from Danny, Mitch stood stock-still in his room, staring at the screen. Then:

Dude, nice timing. She just pulled in.

Without responding, Mitch shoved the phone back in his pocket. Checking the tape deck in the boom box to see that it was loaded and ready to go, Mitch grabbed the boom box, cradling it in his arms like a huge, unwieldy baby.

"Oh man," Mitch muttered to himself. "I should have been training for this."

He bounded down the stairs and back out the front door, still carrying the boom box. It was a twelve-minute ride to Nora's—he'd timed it—so if he hurried, there was no way he'd miss her.

Standing beside his bike, boom box in hand, Mitch realized there was yet another thing he hadn't considered: how he was going to ride while carrying the stupid thing.

"Oh my God," Mitch whispered. "You're killing me, Matlin."

He frantically tore through the sodden cardboard boxes that lined the garage, looking for anything that could help him carry the stereo. In the fifth box, in the corner of the garage, he spied his best option: duct tape.

Mitch stood tall and, holding the boom box with his feeble left hand, ran a strip of duct tape across the front of the boom box and back under his arm. Then he changed hands, grabbed the tape with his left hand

and wrapped it fully around his back, and across the front of the boom box again. A duct tape swaddle for the ugliest, heaviest baby in the world.

Mitch repeated this process again and again, until the roll of tape ran out. He took a few careful steps back towards the bike, and while the boom box jiggled on his stomach, it didn't fall. *Good enough,* he thought.

He climbed onto the bike, gingerly hiked himself up on the seat, put his right foot on the pedal, and pushed off.

Just a few minutes later, Mitch stood at the end of Nora's block, panting and dismounting from the bike. Unsure of how to disassemble the duct tape swaddle, Mitch pushed the boom box away from his body, stretching the straps. He grunted, pushing and pulling and gritting his teeth. A gray Honda Civic came up behind Mitch, and it slowed down beside him. The driver—a middle-aged man with a goatee—rolled down the window and looked out.

"You okay, son?" he asked.

Mitch looked back at him, sweaty and short of breath. "Prom."

The guy smiled. "Been there, brother. Good luck." He rolled up the window and pulled away.

Once he finally broke the bonds of the duct tape, Mitch yanked the stereo away from his chest and held it in his hands. He ripped the duct tape from its face and threw it in the gutter, vowing to pick it back up on his return journey. Holding the boom box under his arm, Mitch walked his bike down the block towards 2005 Girard Avenue, Nora's house.

The Dickinson house had a freshly manicured lawn, which was sopping wet, thanks to the rain. As he set foot on the perfectly trimmed grass, Mitch felt a pang of guilt, but he forced himself to ignore it as he positioned himself under Nora's second-floor window.

Mitch had first seen *Say Anything* at age eleven, and for years it was his favorite movie. John Cusack captures Ione Skye's heart by doing what Mitch was about to do now: standing outside her window, boom box held aloft, blasting her favorite tunes. And as Mitch assumed the position, he got goosebumps. This was it. His whole life was leading up to this very moment.

He pressed play, held the boom box up, and heard the wheels start spinning. After a few crushing seconds of silence, the first song started. And while Mitch didn't know Nora well at all, he was sure that the first song, at the very least, was a winner.

The cheerful, sunny voices of the Hanson brothers bubbled out of the stereo at maximum volume. Mitch hummed along with the song as it started, and then sang along as it continued, trying to create as much volume as possible. After a full thirty seconds of the song, Nora's bedroom window flew open.

"What's going on?" she asked, irritated.

"Nora!" Mitch exclaimed. He couldn't even hear her over the music.

"Hey," she said skeptically. "What's your name again?"

"Nora!" he continued.

"No, what's *your* name?"

"You like Hanson, right?" Mitch yelled, holding

up the boom box even higher. His hands were sweaty; one false move and it could come crashing down on his head.

"What are you doing?" Nora asked.

Realizing he should probably hear what she was saying, Mitch brought down the boom box and turned down the volume knob. "Hey," he said, trying to do his best John Cusack impression.

"You're referencing that movie, right?" Nora asked.

"Yes!" Mitch bellowed gleefully. *She was getting it!*

"What's your name?" she asked.

"Oh yeah, I'm Mitch."

"Mitch what?"

"Mitch Matlin."

". . . Cool." Nora anxiously brushed a few strands of thick auburn hair behind her ear. "So, what's up?"

"Oh yeah, sorry!" Mitch said. "I'm just—um—well, I wanted to ask—"

But before he had a chance to pop the question, he heard a rumbling male voice coming from Nora's direction. Nora heard it too and turned her head behind her.

"Who's out there?" the male voice asked.

Nora said, "Mitch something? I don't know."

"So, anyway," Mitch said loudly, trying to regain her attention. The Hanson brothers were still mmm-bop-ing away on the stereo. *Stupid to start with Hanson.* Mitch cursed himself. *I'll talk slow enough so that it gets to the Toni Braxton song. She can't say no to Toni!*

"Yeah, so anyway," he said again. "I just wanted to ask—um—I'm here to present myself . . . to say that, if you want, but only if you want—I'm not gonna force you, that would be weird . . . ahh, sorry, where am I going with this . . . "

Cutting him off again, the man in the room with Nora revealed himself: Bo Dennis, star linebacker on the football team. Popping his head out of the window, his meaty shoulders and equally meaty head nearly crowded Nora entirely out of the frame.

"Bro, what *is* this?" Bo asked, incredulous. "You're scaring my girl."

Ew, Mitch thought, but stopped himself from saying it out loud. At a loss for words, Mitch could only manage to point at the stereo on the ground. "It's Hanson," he said weakly.

"I know that, and I do like Hanson, but what are you doing here?" Nora asked again.

"Ohh, ohh!" Bo said cheerfully. He laughed loudly, as only someone who thinks he owns the world can laugh. "I think he's trying to ask you to prom, babe." Nora's face lost a shade of its luscious olive tone as she realized Bo was right. Nervously she stared at Mitch, then looked at Bo, then back at Mitch.

She whispered something, and Bo pulled his head back inside the room. Nora looked at Mitch, her lips tightly pursed, looking nauseous. She stammered. "I . . . he . . . "

That was all Nora managed before she pulled her head back into the room and grabbed the window frame. And right as she slid the window back into place and locked it, Toni Braxton started singing, begging her lover to un-break her heart.

Chapter Two

THE NEXT DAY BROUGHT THE SPRING WEATHER everyone in Salt Lake City had been waiting for throughout the month of May. The morning dawned bright and cloudless, and the perfectly yellow sun rose in the east over Grandeur Peak, clearly visible from the Matlins' kitchen window. After a wet, long winter, the regal mountain was green and lush.

But the beauty of the morning was lost on Mitch Matlin as he sat sulking over a cup of lukewarm coffee at the kitchen table. He had barely slept after the miserable encounter with Nora Dickinson the previous afternoon. Or, if he had slept, his dreams were no different than the images and sounds running on repeat through his head.

Ohh, ohh! I think he's trying to ask you to prom, babe.

What's your name again?

I know that, and I do like Hanson, but what are you doing here?

What's your name again?

Mitch shuddered. It wasn't easy to shake off, since he'd been picturing and perfecting his *Say Anything* moment for too many years to remember.

"How 'bout I make you a fresh cup, eh? That looks like sludge," Mitch's dad said, coming up behind him. He put his hands on Mitch's shoulders and gave them a forceful rub.

"Agh, no thanks," Mitch said, arching his back like an irritated tabby cat. "I gotta get going." Mitch got up from the table and grabbed his backpack from the floor. Did it even have his books and notebooks in it? He didn't care to check.

"TGIF, right son?" his dad said cheerfully. "I know yesterday sucked, but let's do something fun this weekend. If the Jazz ever decided to play well enough to get into the playoffs, we would have a basketball game to go to, but—"

"I'll probably just sleep, don't worry about it," Mitch said bitterly, blowing past his dad and out the door.

– – –

After three forgettable morning classes, Kendra made her way into the courtyard at East High to eat her lunch in the sunshine. Though she was in a sour mood, even she had to acknowledge the warmth was soothing. She searched the sprawling grass for Mitch, to no avail. She'd been waiting to see him all morning so they could commiserate about their miserable attempts at getting prom dates the day before. Though they'd texted a bit the night before, Kendra knew he had more to tell her and she him.

As she scanned the grass, Kendra couldn't help but replay the events of the previous afternoon. Every single person had abandoned her in her hour of need! Of course, the apologies and excuses had rolled in to the group thread in the minutes and hours after the end of school (*I couldn't find you!*; *Ugh sorry I had to pee and then I missed you!*; *OMG my grandpa literally died during seventh period, it was srsly so crazy, so sorry girl*). But that didn't make the sting of rejection any easier.

Lost in her reverie, Kendra didn't notice Mitch cutting across the lawn towards her, waving sheepishly. "Forever alone much?" he asked, flicking her forehead.

"Gah!" Kendra sputtered, jerking her head away. "Sorry, I was just a little distracted thinking about the fact that I have no game whatsoever and no one will ever love me."

Smiling ever so slightly, Mitch sat down on the grass and opened his backpack. Immediately he realized he hadn't brought any food. "Of course," he said. "Hard to pack a lunch when you'd rather never eat again and wither away like the pathetic corpse of a human you truly are."

"Well, I can help you there," she said. Mitch

gawked as Kendra pulled out bag after bag of junk food: Oreos, Cheetos, three different flavors of Lay's, and a Tupperware of pizza rolls.

"God, it's like Obese Mary Poppins's handbag," he said.

Kendra tore open the bag of Cheetos and pounded a fistful before saying anything. Mitch took her lead and dove into the package of Oreos. After a minute of desperate eating, Mitch managed a soft, "Thanks."

"I'm pretty good at finding ways to soothe deep internal pain," Kendra said. "I have to do it once a month."

"God, yesterday was awful," Mitch said. And out of nowhere—with his mouth still half full of Oreo—his eyes welled up hot with tears. "I just can't—" he croaked before cutting himself off.

"Yeah, man," Kendra said. "I just sort of stood here after everybody walked away to their buses and stuff. After like ten minutes, the stress wore off and I guess it was good it was raining because nobody could tell I was just, like, openly weeping."

"I don't know why I thought I had a chance," Mitch said. "I mean, honestly. I still haven't managed to get *any* girl to date me. Why did I think Nora Dickinson would have any interest?"

Kendra nodded. "I felt pretty stupid standing here, yesterday," she said softly. "Really stupid."

Mitch looked over at his best friend and their eyes met, each a little damp and red. But he also couldn't help but smile. He marveled at how pathetic his life felt at that moment and how lucky he was to have Kendra in the boat with him.

"You didn't know that Bo Dennis is dating Nora, right?" Mitch asked. "You would have told me?"

"Oh yeah, sorry, forgot to mention my *best friend* Bo Dennis is *shtupping* the love of your life. My bad," Kendra said, chuckling. "Like, what is the appeal of him, anyway? He looks like a thumb."

"Kendra, it's okay, you don't have to comfort me like that."

"You're not hearing me. He's not a boy. He's not human. He's a thumb. And thumbs are ugly."

Mitch sighed, cracking open the pizza rolls. "Well, she likes him for some reason, I guess. Not only am I not cool enough to take Nora Dickinson to prom, I'm not even cool enough to know that I can't!"

"Maybe Adam is dating somebody, too," Kendra said.

"You know," Mitch said softly, "you were probably right."

Kendra looked up, panicked. "About what? Adam *does* have a girlfriend?"

"That I should have asked someone I actually kind of know. That way she would have had to, like, be nice or offer some kind of explanation, or at least say more to me than just 'uh' . . . "

"Well," Kendra started, "Adam didn't say much of anything either. He just said that somebody had already asked him—which was a lie, I asked around— and that he had to go catch his bus, and that he was really sorry. And that we could totally still dance together for, like, one song. So I guess there's that."

This caught Mitch off guard. "Oh. So you're still gonna go?"

"Well, I thought about it," Kendra said. "You *can* go stag, you know."

"Oh my God, but that's social suicide!" Mitch bellowed, nearly choking on a pizza roll. "I'm not gonna let you do that!"

"But dancing with Adam!" Kendra whined, making a pouty face. "He's so hot!"

"It'll be the saddest Cha-Cha Slide you ever slid," Mitch said. "And then it'll be over, and you'll wonder why you came."

Kendra sighed, taking another handful of Cheetos. Her shoulders sank as she imagined that feeling, standing on the dance floor as Adam parted ways with her to go find his *actual* date again. She could picture the cheap colored lights dancing around her feet and in her eyes as she frantically searched the room for the life raft of another friend to dance with—or even just someone else to talk to.

"Maybe we could go together?" Kendra asked. "I guess."

"Wow, try to sound a little *less* enthusiastic," Mitch said. "I don't know, I'm just sort of over the whole thing, to be honest. No offense."

"None taken," Kendra said. "I know exactly what you mean."

A heavy silence hung in the air between them. The dream of prom was flickering out before their eyes.

Mitch looked out around the courtyard at the other East High students enjoying the sunshine and their well-rounded lunches. Suddenly, he felt completely out of place. All the people around the courtyard—many of whom Mitch had known since elementary school—seemed like complete strangers.

"I feel, like, really far away from everyone right now," Kendra said.

"Yes!" Mitch yelled, amazed at how in sync they were. "My thoughts exactly."

Kendra looked at Mitch with a serious gaze. She

took a breath. "You know," she said, "I have kind of a crazy idea."

"Oh boy," Mitch said. "Better hand me those Cheetos."

Kendra did and said, "So, prom is only three days before graduation. And prom is a week from now. So that means we'll be free birds in ten days."

Mitch nodded. "Three plus seven is ten. Couldn't agree with you more."

"So, the other thing," Kendra said, "is that my graduation present is my dad's old Mustang."

Mitch gawked at his best friend, his pulse quickening. "The red one?"

"Yep."

"The 1970?"

"Yep."

"The convertible?"

"Yes. The red 1970 convertible Ford Mustang."

"It's going to be yours."

"Correct."

"In ten days."

"Right again."

"The Mustang."

"Mitch!" Kendra shouted. "So, what if . . . we take a road trip? We get out of here, we put high school in the rearview mirror—"

"Ha, car puns," Mitch said.

"Nice," Kendra said. "We're over this, you and me. Nobody wants us at prom? Fine. We're about to be adults anyway—flying out of the coop, baby, wings spread wide! Let's do something crazy!"

"So our retribution for prom is to take a road trip—not on prom, but after graduation?"

"Exactly," said Kendra. "We'll just tough out prom night, and then we'll have an epic start to our summer that will more than make up for it."

Mitch thought about it silently. "This is all a lot to take in right now. Do you think your parents would let us? That car's kind of old . . . "

"It's been in a garage for twenty years," Kendra said. "It looks totally beautiful, and my dad told me it's in perfect shape. And he knows what he's talking about."

"I'm not sure my parents will let me," Mitch said. "I don't know, Kendra, it sounds cool, but . . . "

"But what?!" Kendra bellowed. "I am *so* not interested in sitting around all summer waiting for college to start so I can forget about how much it sucked getting tossed aside by Adam Green like an old sweater he outgrew. I want to *blast* that feeling away with the top down, flying down the highway! How awesome does that sound?"

Mitch tried to hide the grin creeping across his face, but Kendra spotted it. She sat bolt upright and grabbed Mitch's forearm. "What?!" Mitch jolted backwards.

"We could go to Vegas," Kendra said. She turned her head slowly to look at Mitch, her giddy eyes open wide and her mouth open even wider.

"You look like a Muppet," Mitch said.

"All these lame-os are going to some PG imitation-Vegas where they'll play blackjack for Hershey's Kisses or something," Kendra said. "But what if we do the real thing? Gambling, tanning, gross trashy people from all over the world, the excesses of capitalism around every corner. Doesn't it sound perfect?"

"We're not twenty-one," Mitch said. "We won't be able to do literally any of that."

"Oh, that's *so* NBD," Kendra said. "We can get ourselves some IDs that say otherwise."

"No way, man," Mitch said, "I've seen *Superbad.* I know how that goes."

"We'll come up with something better than McLovin," Kendra said, "I promise. Maybe McLovin, Jr. Oh my God, Mitch, I am obsessed with this. This is happening. We're gonna make some memories—so many memories that we won't have space in our heads to remember this terrible, terrible moment we're living in right now."

Her enthusiasm was infectious. When a small smile crept across his face, Kendra smacked his back like a proud father. "There he is! Matlin is ready to *party!*"

"Yeah," Mitch said. "Yeah, I am. Why not, right? Nobody can stop us. We're out of high school, let's take the bull by the horns. Nora Dickinson and Adam Green don't know what they're missing!"

Kendra held a pizza roll between her fingers, admiring it like a nugget of fourteen-karat gold. "Ten days from now, my boy," she said, "we will be sitting by a glistening pool, surrounded by glistening bodies, all of us lounging in glistening, gilded armchairs . . . eating only the finest pizza rolls the world has to offer."

– – –

"It's only seven hours away," Kendra said, trying not to whine. "That's way less than even going to Grandpa and Grandma's—which I've done alone before, may I remind you, plenty of times!"

"I know, honey, I know," muttered Kendra's mother Angela, rubbing her temples. "And you've reminded us of that plenty of times—just in the last forty-five minutes!"

"This is all a lot to ask of us," said Richard, Kendra's dad, putting his arm around his wife's waist.

"It's hard enough seeing you graduate from high school, and then the next day we're supposed to watch you drive off into the sunset?"

"And what is there to do in Reno, anyway?" Angela asked, exasperated.

Kendra winced. She hated being reminded of the massive lie she was trying to sell to her parents. Though the idea of road tripping to Vegas was something she and Mitch were both dying to do, they quickly realized how difficult it was going to be to actually make it happen. This was one of only a few times in her life Kendra was frustrated by how much her parents cared about her well-being.

In the days since dreaming up the idea, she and Mitch had been working furiously at crafting a story. They had to have all their ducks in a row and tell their parents identical details—down to which freeway they would be taking to get there.

"I told you, my friend Danny's grandma has a huge house there and she's going away for a month. She's, like, *super* rich. Her husband died a while ago, and she took all his money or something. It has one of those infinity pools, a hot tub, a sauna—here, I have pictures, want to see?"

Kendra's parents' eyes opened wide at this offer. Kendra's heart skipped a beat. Were they starting to crack?

She pulled out her phone, where she had ten pictures of different luxurious household amenities—all from ten different homes, collected from a simple Google search. Of course, Mitch had the identical photos.

As Kendra scrolled through, she watched her parents' gaze soften. She was off and running. She pictured Mitch being grilled by his parents at this exact same moment. She hoped he was as good at sticking to the story as she had been. Though her stomach was roiling with anxiety, she was positively serene on the outside.

Danny, Mitch's friend, had no grandmother who lived in Reno. But he promised to field any phone calls from Mitch's or Kendra's parents, if they decided to go above their kids' heads. He said he did a pitch-perfect impression of his own father—who neither Mitch's parents nor Kendra's parents had ever met. Flawless.

"Gosh, it does look nice," Angela said, sighing. "Can we come?" She chuckled at her own joke, looking back at Kendra.

"I don't know," Richard cut in. "I still don't feel good about it."

"What can I say to convince you, Dad?" Kendra asked. "I'll wear my seatbelt. I'll wear ten seatbelts."

"It's that car," he said plainly. "I don't know."

"But you said it's in perfect condition!" Kendra exclaimed. She had been hoping this would not come up. "And you know cars!"

"It's in good shape," Richard said, "but it's not perfect. The gas tank can sometimes be fussy while you're filling it up. You'll have to top it off as far as you can to make sure the thing is full. The hydraulics that move the roof can be sketchy. I'll have to get an outside opinion."

You must be kidding! Kendra wanted to scream. But

instead, she took a deep breath and said, "How long will that take?" Graduation was now only four days away—which meant she and Mitch wanted to hit the road in five.

"What, you got somewhere to be?" Richard raised an eyebrow.

"Reno?" Kendra said. She was genuinely confused. "I told you: Danny's grandma comes back on June 20, so if we want a full week there we have to get going right after graduation."

"We won't even have any time to celebrate!" Angela pleaded.

Kendra wanted to punch a hole in the wall. The whole thing was falling apart again. How was she ever going to convince them?

— — —

"Hey, Mitch, how are ya?" Richard asked, opening the red front door.

"Not too bad, Mr. Brixton," Mitch said, breezing

through the doorway into Kendra's house. "And you?" Mitch knew the key was to be cool and confident with Kendra's parents. That was the only way this was going to work.

"Doing alright, no complaints," her dad said, closing the door. "Kendra? Kendra! Mitch is here!"

"Coming!" came Kendra's voice from upstairs. Mitch knew she'd be a while. That was part of the plan.

"Well, take a seat, why don't you?" Richard said, indicating the brown leather couch Mitch knew very well. He couldn't even begin to count the number of hours he'd spent at the Brixton house over the years.

"Only if you sit with me," Mitch said, winking. Richard obliged and broached exactly the topic of conversation Mitch hoped he would.

"So, talk to me about this road trip," Richard started, the words heavy with skepticism.

Mitch knew this was his moment. He had to project confidence and leave as little room for discussion as possible. "Well, I think it's gonna be a blast," he said.

"I've actually never been to Reno, and this is, like, the perfect excuse—I mean, right? Kendra showed you the pictures, didn't she?"

"Oh, she did," Richard said darkly. "They're quite . . . impressive."

"And thanks so much for letting us use your car!" Mitch exclaimed, beaming. He was determined to talk about the trip as if it was already a sure thing. "That's a really generous gift, Mr. B—to give it to Kendra, and to have its maiden voyage be our little trip out west."

"I'm a little worried about the car, to be honest," Richard said. "I'm not sure it's up to the task."

"But you're the car whisperer!" Mitch said. "Or so I thought . . . " He winked slyly. Mr. Brixton blushed bashfully, like Mitch had just called him the most handsome man on the planet.

"Well, I do know a thing or two," he said.

"My parents are super-psyched about the whole thing," Mitch said. "They both told me about the trips they each took after graduating from high school—and they pale in comparison to this one. I mean, staying in

Danny's grandma's house is one thing, but to get to take this *unreal* car?" Mitch tossed his hands in the air, like he was truly out of words to describe the awesomeness of the trip.

He wasn't lying about this part of it. His parents had been much easier to convince. They had regaled him with stories and told him how jealous they were of his trip to Reno—which, of course, wasn't actually happening. But Mitch took it as an endorsement of the trip anyway.

Kendra came downstairs just as her dad seemed on the verge of giving in. Mitch assumed she'd been listening upstairs, just hidden from view. "What're you guys talking about?" she asked innocently.

Richard looked over at his daughter calmly and sighed. "We're talking about this awesome road trip you guys are going to take."

Chapter Three

*E*VEN BEFORE THEY REACHED THE END OF KENDRA'S block, she felt like she'd been driving the Mustang for years. It handled like a dream and moved so evenly over the asphalt Kendra could have sworn it was levitating a half-inch from the ground. *Hopefully it stays this way,* she thought.

"Woo!" Mitch screamed giddily, slapping the dashboard. The top of the Mustang was down, and the bright Utah sun burned straight down on top of them.

"We haven't even left the neighborhood yet, man," Kendra said, chuckling. "Save it until we're at least out of Salt Lake." She adjusted her classic Ray-Bans on the bridge of her nose, her long black hair flapping glamorously in the breeze.

"I just can't believe we're already doing this!" Mitch said. "Like five days ago, this was a crazy idea we dreamed up—and now it's happening. Hey, thanks for being my friend."

"Oh my God!" Kendra whined. "I'm telling you, save it! We still have something to take care of, my man. Don't count your chickens."

Kendra was right, they did have a big job to take care of. If this didn't work out, their trip to Vegas would be torturously lame—and probably not worth going on at all.

As soon as the plan for the road trip was starting to become a reality, Kendra acted quickly and reached out to one of the most notorious people in their high school class. His name was Austin Lovelace, and he was a provider of all kinds of things high school students couldn't get on their own. And though neither Mitch nor Kendra had ever hit him up for anything before, they needed him for one essential piece of the Vegas puzzle: they needed IDs.

"You made sure he's home, right?" Mitch asked, suddenly less giddy. "If he stiffs us, I swear to God."

"Oh, I'll be pissed. We already gave him a hundred-dollar down payment," Kendra said.

Once the Mustang closed in on Austin's house on Mariposa Avenue, Kendra did as she was told. Austin's instructions were very specific. She pulled over about six houses away from Austin's and kept the motor running.

"Okay," she said to Mitch. Mitch pulled out his phone and typed out the text Austin had instructed to them to send. Want to see a movie tonight?

"Why is that the code?" Mitch asked, pressing SEND.

"It's so if his parents or someone else sees his texts, they won't know anything is up. They'll just think he's really popular."

"Yeah, that he's *really* popular. And that like *every-one* wants to see a movie with him. All on the same night. Austin has a ton of customers. Don't you think that would seem a little suspicious?"

Kendra was about to answer when they spotted Austin, wearing his trademark "Reagan/Bush '84" T-shirt, bounding up alongside them. He opened the rear side door and climbed in.

"'S'up, thugs?" he said. "Hey, wouldja mind putting up the roof? The whole point of this is secrecy, ya know."

"Oh, sorry," Kendra said. Suddenly, it felt like she and Mitch had been dropped into the middle of an episode of *The Wire.* She pressed the button on the control panel that moved the canvas roof. It moved incredibly, excruciatingly slowly.

"So," Austin said hesitantly. "What you guys been up to since graduation?"

"You mean since yesterday?" Mitch asked.

"For sure."

"Not much. Lots of packing, lying to our parents, the usual," Kendra said, winking.

"Man, I feel that!" Austin exclaimed. "This is a

ballsy plan you guys have here, I gotta say. Even Daddy hasn't gotten out to Vegas yet." Kendra shuddered. Austin exclusively referred to himself as "Daddy," and it made her skin crawl.

The roof locked into place above them, and Kendra pulled away from the curb. This was the sketchiest part of the whole plan. Austin insisted they drive around the neighborhood while the deal went down.

"Alright then, cool cats," Austin said, reaching into his pocket. He pulled out two hard plastic cards and handed them to Mitch.

"Oh, they look great!" Kendra said, peeking over from behind the wheel.

Mitch turned them over and over in his hands. They *did* look great. The pictures they sent Austin— taken with their iPhones against the blank wall in a stairwell at school—looked almost identical to the ones on their actual IDs. Mitch read every word on both IDs carefully, looking for spelling errors or anything else. But there were none to be found.

"Make sure Daddy got those birthdays right, yo."

"Yeah, you nailed them," Mitch said. "And these scan?"

"Cross my heart, you bet, man," Austin said. "Daddy uses the one Daddy made for himself all over the place. Run that barcode through anywhere, and it'll pass. Scout's honor."

"We can't thank you enough, Austin," Kendra said. "How much do we owe you?"

"Just another hundo, if you don't mind," he said. "Or even if you *do* mind. Either way, Daddy just wants his money."

Mitch reached into the glove compartment and pulled out five twenties, handing them to Austin. They had made a point of taking a trip to an ATM on the way to Austin's house, so that they didn't have to charge their debit cards at all in Vegas. With just one charge from Las Vegas on their monthly bill, all of the lies and deception would be laid bare—and who knew what kind of punishment either Mitch's or Kendra's parents would mete out.

"*Muchas gracias,* my people!" Austin crowed.

"We owe you one, man. We'll send you some pics from the casinos we get into out there, thanks to you."

"Ooh yeah, don't do that," Austin said edgily. "No paper trail, no digital trail, no nothing. Daddy's gotta protect that reputation, you know? Next time we chill, you can show me, but I don't want to get tied up in anything, you got me?"

Mitch was thrown off, but knew better than to push his luck with a true professional. "You got it, man."

Kendra pulled up onto Austin's block and put the car in park. "Stay safe," Austin said as he climbed out. "Don't do anything Daddy wouldn't do."

– – –

The drive out of Salt Lake City and into central Utah breezed by. Under the high, cloudless sky, Interstate 15 took the old red Mustang through a series of different landscapes, each more staggering than the next. Steep, craggy mountains gave way to flat expanses of desert floor, where the brick-red rocks continued so far into the distance that they looked like they stretched out beyond the ends of the Earth.

Though Mitch and Kendra had started out the drive laughing and giddily celebrating the sheer fact that they were actually on the road, they quickly fell silent as the natural world blossomed around them. Mitch sat quietly in the passenger seat, his elbow on the door near the window. His chin sat comfortably in the palm of his hand as he stared out at the barren wilderness, devoid of life except for thick pine forests on the highest mountain peaks and a few vultures circling high overhead.

"It's hard to look at all of this and *not* start thinking about the meaning of life," Mitch said softly. A few moments of silence went by before he looked over at Kendra. She glanced back at him from the road.

"What?" she asked, startled. "Did you say something?"

"Yeah, exactly," Mitch said, smiling. Even just an hour into the six-hour journey, Mitch felt like they were a million miles from home. And though Mitch had taken trips with his family to explore the wilds of Utah, it had been a while. Besides, Mitch thought, it's entirely different doing it with your best friend, without your family around at all.

Without your family around at all. The words echoed inside his head, booming and somewhat sinister. He couldn't help but wonder, was this a good idea? Not only were neither his nor Kendra's family nearby, they didn't actually know where their children were! Reno was in completely the other direction from where they were headed. The rough landscape of rural Utah— which looked like the set of an old country western movie, more and more every second—seemed a little threatening.

"Man," Kendra said, apropos of nothing. "I'm just so crazy excited to be doing this. This is so ballsy, dude—we are living on the edge! Even crazy Austin Lovelace hasn't done anything like this before!" Her happiness was totally pure, Mitch could tell. He tried to gin up some carefree giddiness in himself.

"Yeah!" he said, a little too forcefully. Then he couldn't think of anything else to say.

Kendra saw right through it, obviously. "You okay, dude?" she asked. "You've gone a little quiet."

Mitch sighed, looking over at his friend for the first time in a while. "I don't know. I just feel intimidated all of a sudden."

"Intimidated? By what?"

"I don't know, I just . . . this *is* ballsy, you're right. And, like, look at where we are. We're out in the middle of nowhere. What if something bad happens?"

Kendra laughed, relaxing. "Oh my God, dude, you are *such* a Debbie Downer right now. This was all part of the plan! We are getting *out*. Think of all those lame little ducklings back home. They all peaked last weekend at prom! They all put on their boutonnieres and the whatever-the-dumb-things-the-girls-have-to-wear-are-called, and they got all anxious and stressed out and caked themselves in makeup, and they tried *so* hard to have 'the best night of their lives, OMG!'

"What we're doing right now, this is what people

actually want to be doing. We're doing something crazy. Prom is the opposite of crazy. I mean, honestly, did anyone actually have a *magical night*? No! They all were either too messed up or not messed up enough, they either grinded on each other for three hours or they wish they had, and then they all went home alone. Seriously!"

Mitch could only smile at Kendra's rant. She was at her best when she was like this. She could change your view of the world in a second. "Yeah," he said. "You're for sure right."

"I know I am!"

"You've never even been to prom though," Mitch said. "How are you so sure about all this stuff?"

"Because I've been to high school, man," Kendra said. "And so have you. And I've been to other dances, and they were all equally disappointing. The only difference is that by the time senior prom rolls around, you basically know everybody there, and chances are you don't really like most of them." Kendra didn't have a ton of friends, but she didn't seem to mind. She liked observing people from a distance just fine.

About half a mile ahead of them, Mitch could see a car pulled over on the shoulder of the four-lane highway. As the Mustang sped towards it, Mitch studied the scene: a desperate-looking middle-aged guy stood in front of his plain-looking sedan that was belching huge amounts of steam out of the hood.

"Jeez," Kendra said, looking at the guy and his pathetic situation. "That looks awful, to be alone out here with your car completely giving up on you. I hope he has cell service."

She was right, it did look awful. Though they were still on the interstate, there weren't any major towns around. The last road sign Mitch remembered seeing was for a town called Levan, population 854.

— — —

"This looks like as good a joint as any," Kendra said,

pulling into the parking lot of Lauren's Famous Roadside BBQ Pit. "Yeah?"

"Totally," Mitch said. "I'm starving."

Kendra rolled into a space and put the car in park. Before turning off the ignition, she checked the all-important dial on the control panel. "Remind me to get gas before we leave town," she said.

"Aye aye, captain," said Mitch.

The restaurant was exactly what Kendra had hoped it'd be: a dimly lit, hazy diner with worn red vinyl booths. A few lone men and one couple sat scattered around the huge dining room.

"Hey there, kids," said a cheerful middle-aged hostess coming up to them. "You old enough to be in here?"

Kendra's heart skipped a beat. "Oh," she said awkwardly. "Is there . . . do we have to . . . ID?"

The woman guffawed. "I'm kiddin', I'm kiddin'! Everybody's welcome here," she said, grabbing some menus. Then suddenly she shot both Mitch and Kendra a searing glare. "Unless you're vegetarians."

Mitch and Kendra fell silent again, too stunned to talk. Then the woman threw back her head and cackled again, louder than before. "Y'all gotta loosen up! Let's get some ribs in you, then you'll laugh at my jokes."

Mitch and Kendra sat in a booth near the window. Kendra was grateful for the opportunity to look out on the parking lot and keep track of the car. It was nicer than anything else out in the lot—by a mile—and who knew what kind of people lurked out there.

As she and Mitch looked over the menus—loosely bound yellowed pages dotted with "Lauren's Special Secret Homemade Finger-Lickin' Cattle Sauce"— Kendra told herself to relax. She had focused on calming Mitch down in the car, but now that she was able to be honest with herself, Kendra realized she was sort of anxious, too.

Though her dad was certain—"Cross my heart, hope to die—me, not you," as he said—the car was ready to take on a trip like this, Kendra would only be convinced once they got it all the way back to Salt Lake. It was handling fine, and the engine was motoring as fast as she wanted it to be, but with every uphill climb—and every time the engine temperature gauge crept up another notch—she got a tiny anxious tingle at the base of her spine.

The trip would come to a screeching halt if the car broke down—as would her summer, as would her parents' faith in her.

But before she could ruminate any further, their waiter—a tall muscle-bound blond guy not much older than Kendra and Mitch—appeared beside the table. "Know what you want?" he asked.

"Absolutely," Mitch said. "Just mac and cheese for me, please."

The waiter nodded his head. "You got it, bud." He turned toward Kendra.

"And what's your name?" Kendra asked, turning on the charm. She never waited around to be flirted with, she was always happy to lead the charge.

"Oh boy," Mitch muttered under his breath.

"Laurence," the waiter said happily, his smile revealing gleaming white teeth.

Kendra laughed. "No, it's not."

He stared back, his smile fading in confusion. "Yes . . . yes it is?" He pointed to his nametag where, indeed, it said *Laurence*.

"Isn't this place called Lauren's?" Kendra asked, trying to keep the charm flowing.

"Yeah! That's my momma."

"Ah," Kendra said. "Doesn't that get, like, *really* confusing?"

The waiter shrugged, but said nothing.

"Probably would have gone with Lorenzo," Kendra muttered, smirking.

Mitch cleared his throat. "Kendra."

She looked up at Laurence, who was waiting patiently for her order. "What do you recommend?" Kendra asked pleasantly.

Laurence was all too happy to answer this question, flashing that Hollywood smile again. His upper arms stretched the fabric of his starchy white sleeves, and every so often his pale blue eyes met Kendra's as he listed off his favorite items on the menu. Laurence was talking, but Kendra wasn't listening; she was fantasizing about this Viking in front of her. Then suddenly, Laurence stopped talking.

"Uh . . . " Kendra said, caught off guard. "I'll have that."

Laurence stared at her, confused. "Which one? The rib tips or the Ultimate Pork Sandwich?"

"Oh," Kendra said. "Let's try that sandwich." Whatever it was, it sounded challenging. *And guys respect a warrior,* Kendra thought.

Laurence marked it down on his notepad, pivoted, and walked away. Kendra gazed after him, until Mitch snapped his fingers in her face, chuckling. "Jeez, keep it in your pants, Romeo!" he whispered sharply.

Kendra groaned. "He's so cute, I couldn't help it. I'm on vacation, let a girl have a little fun."

When Laurence came back with two glasses of water, Kendra tried to keep the conversation flowing. "So, your mom doesn't come into work much anymore?"

Laurence's expression darkened. "Well, she's passed

on now, and so my aunt is the majority owner, and in a little while it'll be mine, I guess."

Kendra frowned. "I'm sorry about your mom," she said. "I can't imagine."

Laurence nodded bashfully. "Yeah, thanks."

"But it's cool about this place," Kendra said. "I mean, you get to eat delicious food all the time, for free." Now that she was trying to hook Laurence with every word, Kendra reprimanded herself constantly. *What if he doesn't like barbecue? Dumb idiot!*

"Yeah, you're right," he said, though some sadness had crept into his voice. "Anyway, y'all from around here, or what?"

"Salt Lake," Mitch said. "Not far, but . . . "

"Different world over there," Laurence said. "Never been up that way. I keep meaning to, but you know how it goes."

"We're on our way to Vegas, actually," Kendra said.

"Vegas?" Laurence asked, obviously confused. "Aren't y'all Mormon? Isn't that against y'all's way of life?"

68

Mitch laughed. "No, we're not. But even if we were, I think we could still go to Vegas. Right?"

Kendra shrugged. She knew next to nothing about Mormonism. Even though a fair amount of kids at East High were Mormon, and she passed by the Mormon Temple most days, it hadn't ever been a part of her life, or Mitch's.

"Are y'all twenty-one?" Laurence asked. "I'm not, and you don't look much older than me."

"No, we just graduated high school," Kendra said. Then, too quickly, she added, "But we're eighteen!" *What?!* Kendra wanted to slap herself. *You think that's what he wants to hear? Talking about how you're a barely legal adult? Get it together!*

"Cool," Laurence said, blushing a little.

Mitch swooped in, trying to rescue the conversation for all of their sakes. "We're just trying to cut loose a little. We graduated, we're out of there, we're both headed to the U in the fall, but we want to live a little. You know?"

Even Kendra could recognize this was not the right

thing to say. From what Laurence already said, it was clear that even if he knew the feeling, he definitely didn't have the money or time to act on it.

Laurence paused, unsure of what to say. "Well, that's cool," he managed. "This restaurant's a pretty big job. My momma didn't take a vacation for thirty years, and I think my aunt is gonna do the same thing, maybe even longer."

"Well, let me talk to her, maybe I can convince her to let you come with us," Kendra said. As soon as the words left her mouth, Mitch gave her a swift kick in the shin under the table. Kendra winced, but smiled up at Laurence as if nothing was wrong.

Laurence shook his head a little, looking down at his feet. "Maybe another time," he said. "I'll go check on your food."

The sandwich that Kendra had ordered was more of a challenge than she could have possibly imagined. A hefty brioche bun was chock-full of chopped barbecue pork, layered with jalapenos and multiple strips of thick-cut bacon—and everything was drenched with barbecue sauce and melted American cheese. Laurence put the plate down in front of her and looked directly into Kendra's eyes. "Good luck."

As he walked away, Kendra turned excitedly to Mitch. "Oh, he's so into me." Kendra picked up the sandwich—or tried, desperately grasping onto it as the sodden bread sagged. "This is for you, baby," she said, practically throwing her face straight into it.

Mitch smiled, daintily eating his mac and cheese. "Adam Green doesn't know what he's missing."

– – –

Forty-five minutes later, Mitch was behind the wheel of the Mustang, angling slowly towards the exit of the gas station. Luckily he had remembered Kendra's directive to get gas before hitting the road again, since she was distracted by other thoughts.

As he made the turn out of the parking lot, Mitch glanced over at Kendra, who had leaned the passenger seat as far backward as possible, and was stretched out like a patient in a sickbed. She groaned, clutching her stomach. "Why didn't you stop me?" she bellowed. "I feel like I ate an entire slaughterhouse."

Mitch smiled. "But at least Laurence will love you for it. Think about it this way, this'll just be a fun story to tell your three adorable children while they're bouncing on your knees in your million-dollar mansion out here in the desert. 'Mommy won me over by shoving three whole pigs into her face. It was the most beautiful thing I've ever seen anyone do. I knew right then and there she was the love of my life.'"

"Ugh, shut *up!*" Kendra whined.

"You did leave him your number, right?" Mitch asked.

Kendra whipped her eyes open wide at Mitch. "Of course I did! God, you actually think I have zero game."

"We can come right back here on the way home," Mitch said. "You'll just have to order a salad next time." Mitch leaned forward in his seat as they began merging back onto Interstate 15, checking for other cars. Luckily, traffic was light.

"Oh, don't worry, I'm never eating again," Kendra moaned. "Unless Laurence liked what he saw, and he wants me to eat that horrible sandwich every day for the rest of my life. I'd bathe in barbecue sauce for him. But for now, I'm going to sleep." With that, Kendra pulled the hood of her sweatshirt over her eyes and rolled into the fetal position.

Mitch smiled over at her, thankful that he had chosen to go on *this* adventure with *this* friend. It was still daunting, but at least they were here together. No matter what ended up happening, they'd have a lifetime of memories to show for it. Memories and stories just like his parents had. Stories of a kid finally lighting out into the world, taking it by the horns, staking his place in it as an adult.

The Mustang hurtled forward into the sunbaked desert, towards more uphill climbs and breathtaking vistas, towards less and less civilization.

Lost in thought, Mitch didn't notice the needle on the gas meter was only halfway toward full.

Chapter Four

THE SUN WAS JUST BARELY GONE FROM THE SKY AS the red Mustang closed in on Las Vegas. There had been a few stars blinking as it darkened around them, but seemingly with every foot closer to Sin City, they disappeared, clouded by who knew what—the bright lights, the smog, the haze of debauchery.

"Hey," Mitch said, rubbing Kendra's shoulder. "You should see this."

Kendra stirred, now closing in on hour three of her post-barbecue nap. Slowly, her eyes opened and she looked up at Mitch. "Are we . . . " she started sleepily, but her eyes settled closed again.

"Yo!" Mitch shouted. Kendra jerked straight up as if Mitch had thrown ice-cold water into her face.

"What, what, what is it?" she stammered, panicked.

"Just look," Mitch said, smiling. Kendra sat up and looked straight ahead of them.

The lights of the Las Vegas Strip shimmered ahead of them, a visual cacophony of colors and roving lights. As if someone had dropped a pile of gemstones— rubies, emeralds, opals, topazes—into the desert, and lit them on fire.

"Holy moly," Kendra whispered. "This is . . . "

"Even better than you thought?" Mitch said. "I know."

Mitch and Kendra giddily pointed out the individual hotels and casinos along Las Vegas Boulevard as I-15 bent around southward, running parallel to the Strip. There was the giant faux big top of Circus Circus, the gold, brick-shaped Trump International Hotel—"And there's where we *won't* be going," Kendra said, proudly thumbing her nose—the iconic arched bridge of the Venetian, the monolithic temple of Caesar's Palace, and the majestic Bellagio.

"Oh, wait a second," Mitch said suddenly. "We don't know where we're staying."

Kendra guffawed, slapping the dashboard in front of her. "Oh my God! We're idiots!" she cried.

Mitch's heart rate went up sharply as he realized, at sixty-five miles an hour, they were at risk of blowing by the Strip entirely. They had to act fast. "Google 'cheap Vegas hotels' or something?" he said frantically.

"Just get off at the next exit," Kendra said, "and we can pull over and do some research."

Mitch did as he was told, angling the Mustang towards the exit for Tropicana Avenue. It was only then, as he looked at the blinking turn light, that he noticed something else illuminated on the control panel: the empty light.

"Oh my God, what?" Mitch exclaimed. "I totally filled that up after lunch!"

Kendra's heart practically stopped. "How long has that been on?"

"I don't know," Mitch said.

"Did you top it off?" Kendra asked. "My dad warned me it might cut off a few times before it's full and you have to keep going . . . oh my God, did I not tell you that?"

The Mustang was flying up the exit ramp towards Tropicana Avenue, coming to a stoplight next to a strip club called the American Dream. Normally Mitch would have cracked a joke, but there wasn't time. "Which way should I turn?" Mitch asked frantically.

"Um . . . to the right," Kendra said. "I don't know!"

Mitch turned anyway, and after a few blocks spotted a beacon of hope: a Hampton Inn & Suites not more than a hundred feet away. "I'm gonna pull in there," Mitch said. "We don't have to stay there, but this could be perfect."

He pulled into a turn lane on Tropicana Avenue, putting his blinker on and waiting for the opposite-side traffic to abate. "An oasis in the desert," Kendra said as Mitch had enough room to turn.

But as soon as he made the turn, Mitch knew

something was up. The car suddenly had no momentum; it was barely moving across the busy four-lane road! Mitch pumped the pedal—once, twice, three times—as the headlights of oncoming cars loomed through Kendra's window.

"What's happening?" Kendra shouted.

"It's dying!" Mitch screamed, fighting away the feeling of imminent death creeping into his head.

Then, on one frantic shove of the gas pedal, the car sprang to life, lurching forward the remaining ten feet into the driveway of the hotel. But once the rear of the car had barely crossed the threshold, inches from being hit by a huge black SUV flying down the road, the engine completely died.

"You've gotta be *kidding me*," Mitch spat, bitterly throwing the gearshift into park.

"What do we do?" Kendra asked, her voice trembling with fear. Just as Mitch was about to confess his complete ignorance and fear, two voices came careening across the parking lot.

"Hey!" the two voices, both female, shouted together. "Do you need help?"

Mitch rolled down his window and leaned his head out. "Yes!"

The two women walked briskly across the parking lot. As they got closer to the car, the car's headlights illuminated them. They both looked to be in their late twenties and were dressed to go out on the town, by the looks of it. They each wore tight, short cocktail dresses and had stilettos on their feet.

"Your car die?" asked one of the women, coming up to the window. She was a stunning black woman with straightened jet-black hair streaked with cobalt.

"Looks that way," Mitch said abashedly.

The woman laughed. "You're like thirty feet from the finish line!" She laughed loudly, her dark-red lips pulling back to reveal gleaming white, perfectly aligned teeth. She was a lot for Mitch to take in. He gawked up at her, slouched in the driver's seat.

"Pretty pathetic, huh?" Kendra said from the passenger side.

The woman locked eyes with Mitch, not acknowl-edging Kendra's comment. He felt paralyzed by her gaze, which was serious but not threatening. Mitch felt like she was trying to tell him a secret.

"I'm Patrice," the woman said, extending her hand. Mitch took it and shook, smiling dumbly. After a pause, Kendra leaned over to look Patrice in the eye.

"He's Mitch," Kendra said flatly, "and my name's Kendra."

"Oh. Yeah," Mitch muttered, smiling sheepishly.

"I'll touch you," Patrice said. Mitch's eyes flew open comically, his heart pounding.

"What?!" he exploded, sweat breaking out on the base of his neck.

"I said we'll push you," Patrice said again, slowly.

"Oh," Mitch said, his face suddenly boiling hot.

Kendra again saved his neck. "That'd be great," she said charmingly. "What do you need us to do?"

Patrice's friend, who sported shoulder-length platinum-blonde hair and dangling pendant ear-rings, sauntered up behind her. "I'm Abby," she said, extending her hand towards Mitch. He took it, noticing how warm her long slender fingers were.

This time, Patrice filled in the blanks. "He's Mitch," she said, winking back at him.

"And he's not as dumb as he looks," Kendra piped in dryly. "I mean . . . not usually."

"No problem," Abby said. "I'd say dumb guys are my type."

What is going on?! Mitch screamed inside his head. He wanted to high five Kendra a million times in a row. They'd been in Vegas for ten minutes and already two gorgeous women were coming onto him!

"Here," Patrice said, looking at Kendra, "why don't you get out, and the three of us will push?"

"Totally," Kendra said, throwing the door open. Mitch was sure that was passive-aggressive code for *Turn off your teenage-boy brain and make sure we don't get blown to smithereens by the cars flying at thirty miles an hour, five feet away from us!*

Mitch watched in the rearview mirror as the three of them got behind the bumper. "Ready!" Kendra yelled.

After a moment, Mitch realized he didn't ask one very important question. "What do I do . . . ?" he asked dumbly.

"Oh my *God!*" Kendra shouted. "Put it in neutral!" Abby and Patrice laughed. *Great,* Mitch thought, *there go my chances with those two. Nice going, Matlin.*

Mitch moved the gearshift into neutral. "Okay!" he shouted, putting his hands on the steering wheel. And then . . . nothing happened. Mitch heard groans of agony from behind the car. He waited five seconds . . . ten seconds . . . still nothing. "Hey, maybe I should push instead!" he shouted out the window.

"Shut up!" Abby yelled, smirking. "Girl power!" With one huge push, the women started the car rolling across the asphalt. Mitch kept his hands on the steering wheel.

"You're doing awesome!" he cheered.

"Little to the left!" Patrice yelled from behind. Mitch did as he was told, angling the Mustang toward a parking spot coming ever closer.

With a few more grunts and groans, Abby, Patrice,

and Kendra successfully pushed the car into the spot, precisely between the two white lines.

"Woo!" Mitch cheered, moving the gearshift back into park and tossing off his seatbelt. He jumped out of the car and jogged to the bumper, where the women were leaning over, catching their breath with their hands on their knees.

"Great work, guys," Mitch said. Now that he was standing, he could really appreciate just how tall Abby and Patrice were. In their six-inch heels, they stood three or four inches above him. *I thought I only liked girls who were shorter than me,* he thought. *Guess I thought wrong.*

"What's that saying about Ginger Rogers?" Patrice asked.

"She did everything Fred Astaire did—only backwards and in heels," Abby said, smiling and readjusting her hair.

"Yass!" Patrice cheered, fist-bumping Abby and Kendra. "That is so us right now."

"Do these count?" Kendra asked, indicating her fashionable Puma hi-top sneakers.

"It's a more holistic thing," Abby said.

Patrice nodded. "Yeah, in our society, all women are *always* walking backwards in heels, you know? Metaphorically?"

Kendra nodded skeptically.

"Tooootally," Mitch said, trying to butt in. "I am *right* there with you." Kendra rolled her eyes so far back Mitch thought they might disappear into her skull.

"Well, anyway," Abby said, "there you guys go. You're not getting killed in traffic tonight."

"Thank you guys so much," Mitch said, coming closer to them. "We owe you. Seriously, big time."

"Yeah, what can we do for you?" Kendra asked. "We could buy you dinner or . . . "

"No, no," Patrice said. "No need for any of that. We wanted to help."

Abby nodded. "Our pleasure, seriously. But we're going over to MGM. Are you guys going out?"

Mitch and Kendra looked at each other, desperately trying to communicate in silence. Finally, Kendra said, "Maybe in a bit. Gotta . . . get unpacked, you know?"

Patrice smiled. "I feel you. Here, Mitch, give me your phone." Mitch's heart practically rocketed out of his chest as he took out his iPhone. Patrice snatched it and typed in her number.

Handing the phone back to him, she smiled—a subtle smirk that Mitch felt was just for him. "There you go, now you can hit us up whenever you want. I just texted myself from your phone, so I have you, too. We'll be together all night," Patrice said.

Who's "we"? Mitch wanted to scream. *You and Abby? Me and you? Me and you and Abby?*

But Abby and Patrice were already waving goodbye, walking across the parking lot. "Our Uber is here!" Abby called. "See you guys soon!"

Then they ducked into a black Honda and were gone, heading down Tropicana Avenue, over the highway overpass, and out onto Las Vegas Boulevard.

Mitch and Kendra watched them go in complete

silence. After the Honda disappeared over the crest of the highway overpass, they turned to look at each other.

"What just happened?" Mitch whispered.

− − −

"Alright, could be worse!" Kendra cheered as she turned on the hotel room's lights. Two double beds sat side by side, separated by a tiny tan bedside table. On top of the table sat an old digital alarm clock, blinking 12:00 in bright red numerals.

"Smells a little like smoke," Mitch said, tossing his duffel bag on the bed.

"Well, how long ago do you think it was legal to smoke in hotels here? Like, until yesterday?" Kendra said, smirking. Mitch shrugged and tossed himself down on the bed.

"Man, I'm exhausted," he groaned towards the ceiling. "This day was epic."

"You didn't *seem* too exhausted with Abby and

Patrice," Kendra said, doing cartoonish hair flips and duck faces while saying the girls' names. "I thought I was going to have to put a freaking leash on you."

Mitch sat up slightly and looked at Kendra, smiling. "Patrice was totally flirting with me, though, be honest."

"Oh my *God!*" Kendra shouted. "He's still at it! Dude, if they thought you were cute at first, they definitely don't now. You had literally zero chill."

"She gave me her number!" Mitch was indignant. How could Kendra not see what he was seeing?

"That was a power play," Kendra said, shrugging. "Trust me, man. Girls are tricky like that. She was just getting off on seeing you sit there at her feet like a little golden retriever."

His blood pulsing, Mitch flopped back down onto the mattress. He was at a loss for words. He didn't remember the last time his best friend had been so cold and dismissive of him. *I laughed along with you and encouraged you with that stupid waiter,* Mitch thought. *Why not return the favor?*

"So, what happened with the car, man?" Kendra asked.

Now you're accusing me of that too? Mitch wanted to say. "I mean, either it started burning up fuel like crazy, or it was the problem that you didn't tell me about."

Kendra chuckled bitterly. "So, it's my fault?"

"Whoa," Mitch said, "I didn't say that."

"I just can't believe we screwed up that bad. Already." Kendra put her face in her hands. "What if that thing is permanently dead? Oh my God."

"It's not. It can't be," Mitch said. "We just have to get some more gas in it. Maybe we'll have to get it towed? I don't know how these things work."

But Kendra wasn't listening. It was like she had already given up on the entire trip.

Suddenly Kendra's phone sprang to life, chirping loudly as it rang. "Oh no," she said, like she'd just gotten a life-threatening diagnosis. "It's my parents."

Mitch's eyes flew over to her, his hair standing

straight up on his neck. "You have to answer it," he said. "If you don't, they'll think you're dead."

"Okay, but help me along the way. Make sure I don't say anything stupid." Mitch nodded gravely, taking a deep breath. Both he and Kendra knew that if they dropped the ball, this entire thing could be over in an instant.

"Hello?" Kendra asked.

"Hey, hey!" came her dad's voice from the other end of the line. "Thought you weren't gonna answer there for a second."

"Nope, I'm here," Kendra said, forcing a smile.

"Mom's here, too," Richard said. "Say something, honey."

"Hi, sweetness," Angela crooned. "How are you? You've made it to Reno by now, or are you still on the road?"

"Nope, we're here!" Kendra said. "Just got in a few minutes ago, actually. Good timing!" She was really trying to sound happy. From across the room, Mitch took a big deep breath and made a big show of pushing his hands downward, in a "keep cool" gesture.

"How was the drive?" Angela asked.

Before she could answer, Kendra heard her dad in the background. "Honey, put me on speakerphone."

Then her mom, muttering, "I don't know how to—"

"Just give it to me, here, I'll do—"

"Don't order me around like that, Richard, you *know* I don't like it when you do that—"

As they squabbled, Kendra took a deep breath.

"Alright, can you hear us?" Richard asked on the other end of the line.

"Yep, sure can," Kendra said.

"Okay, so how was the drive?"

"Totally nice, really not much traffic."

"And which route did you take? Looked like there were a few options."

Kendra's blood ran cold. She pointed at Mitch, mouthing *Your phone! I need your phone!* Mitch grabbed it and tossed it across to her. "What's that?"

she said, filling time. She unlocked the phone and opened Maps.

"I said which route did you take?" Richard asked, spelling out each word deliberately. Kendra searched for a route between Salt Lake City and Reno. The phone thought, and thought, and thought . . . *Come on!* Kendra wanted to scream.

"Uh," she said, "let's see. It was mostly on the—" Just then the map filled out and showed the route. "It was mostly on Highway Eighty," she said, breathing a tiny sigh of relief. One more second of indecision and it would have been totally obvious she had no idea.

"Ah, sure, on the interstate," Angela said. "Most efficient, I guess."

"Yep," Kendra said, unsure of what to add.

"You make any stops?" Richard asked. "I hope so! It's not safe to drive for more than a few hours at a time, I've found. Your eyes start crossing and all that. You're not really *seeing* the road anymore."

"Oh, absolutely," Kendra said. Frantically she searched around the route for a name of a town to feed her parents. "Yeah we stopped in . . . Elko. Elko, Nevada?"

"Ah, Elko!" Angela said enthusiastically. "We've been there, Richard, haven't we?"

"Oh, you remember, honey . . . " Richard began. While he rambled on about some story that didn't involve her, Kendra allowed herself to relax. The talk was going well. There was no way they suspected anything. She smiled at Mitch across the room, giving him a cheerful "Okay" with her index finger and thumb.

"Kendra?" her mom asked.

"Oh! What?" she asked, flustered.

"Are you alright, hon? You seem a little distant or something," Richard said. Then his voice got low and serious as he said, "Honey, if there are drugs or alcohol there and you've imbibed just say the word. We won't be mad, we won't be judgmental, we just want you to be safe—"

"Whoa, whoa!" Kendra said. "No, nothing like that. Just . . . tired."

"Well, sure," Angela said. Kendra could practically

hear her mom patting her dad's leg, telling him to calm down. "So, did you get any lunch along the way or anything?"

Kendra's mouth started moving before she could stop it. "Yes! We went to this awesome barbecue place off the highway. It was called Lauren's or something—is that right, Mitch?"

Mitch's jaw dropped and his face turned white. Only then did it click in for Kendra what she had just done. The odds were definitely zilch that there was *another* barbecue restaurant in Elko—or anywhere in Utah *or* Nevada—called Lauren's. She frantically tried to fix her mistake: "Or, maybe, I don't remember what it was called . . . Lauren's doesn't sound quite right, all of a sudden. I don't know!"

Mitch looked like he was going to have a panic attack. He flopped backwards on the bed, putting his hands over his face.

"I'll look it up," Richard said. "If it's so good, maybe your mom and I will take our *own* road trip out there to go try it!"

"It was Lauren's, you said?" Angela asked cheerfully.

"No, you know . . . that doesn't sound right anymore," Kendra spat. "I'll have to look it up again. I don't know where Lauren's came from!" She laughed nervously, trying to find something else to talk about. "The car is holding up great, Dad. No worries there." Her heart sank. She could handle lying about the other stuff. But lying about the car was too much.

"Oh, excellent!" he cheered. The distraction worked.

"Yep, the steering is really smooth and it really has some get-up-and-go!"

Kendra could hear her dad slap his knee in the background. He did that only when he was at his absolute happiest—when the Utes won a football game, or when Bill Maher was on TV. "Your mom was nervous," he said. "See, honey? Nothing to be nervous about!"

"Well, I'll withhold judgment until that car and that girl are back in our driveway," she said. "But until then . . . " She trailed off, her voice trembling.

"Oh, mom," Kendra said, trying not to sound totally exasperated. "We're going to be fine! The trip out here was seriously *so* easy." Her heart sank saying it. It *had* been easy—up until the last few feet, when she and Mitch's stupidity had almost cost them the car and their lives.

"I know you'll be fine," Angela said, sniffling. "You're a very self-assured young woman, and Mitch is a great copilot."

"Exactly," Kendra said, trying to pull herself together. "Nothing to worry about whatsoever."

There was a lull in the conversation, so Kendra jumped on it. "Well, guys, I should sign off. We're gonna take a dip in the pool and make some s'mores."

Mitch gave her a thumbs-up from where he lay across the room.

"Ooh, sounds fun," Angela mused. "Honey, maybe *we* should make s'mores!"

"I'm on Atkins again, but you should certainly go ahead, honey," Richard said. Kendra rolled her eyes, worried this would send her parents into another downward spiral of useless conversation. But her dad managed to stay on track. "Have a good night and get some sleep, alright? We don't want you coming back too tired."

Normally Kendra would mock her dad for saying something like that—as if she weren't an adult who could take care of herself!—but she decided against it for the time being. "Will do," she said calmly. "I promise."

"Goodnight, sweet cheeks," Richard said. "Say hi to Mitch for us!" Both of them frantically blew kisses into the phone.

"Love you, bye," Kendra said quickly before they could say anything else. She hung up and tossed the phone onto the floor, sighing violently.

"Not bad," Mitch said.

"I know, I know," Kendra said. "I screwed up with the barbecue thing. You don't have to tell me."

Mitch threw his arms out wide. "I wasn't going to!"

"Sorry," Kendra said. "That was just stressful. And I'm exhausted. I'm not a lot of fun right now."

"Me neither," Mitch said. "You hungry?"

"Not in the least," Kendra said, smiling. "But I'll come with you if you want to get something."

"There's an In-N-Out across the street," Mitch said. "I'll walk over there and get something for myself."

Without another word, Mitch got up from the bed and walked out the door. Kendra thought about shouting after him and telling him to stay. But the words didn't come.

Chapter Five

THE NEXT MORNING DAWNED HAZY AND DANK. THE air was heavy with steam rising off the concrete sprawl of the Strip and its surroundings. Kendra stood just outside the hotel, already marinating in the stifling air. She swatted at a bead of sweat trickling down the nape of her neck, gritting her teeth. *It's already above ninety and it's barely 9 a.m.,* she mused.

The night before, almost as soon as Mitch had left the room, Kendra erupted into a fit of tears and moans, doubling over on the mattress and sobbing like a heartbroken middle schooler. The wave of emotion had shocked her. And while crying felt good and helped her fall asleep just minutes later, she could not make heads or tails of what she was feeling. Was it the stress of the Mustang? Was she missing her family? Was she just *now* experiencing the sadness of being rejected by Adam Green? Was she afraid? Did she hate Mitch? Even now, hours later, she wasn't sure what had come over her.

But one thing was for sure: thanks to the exhaustion of the day, she had slept like a log. When the glare of the desert sun woke her up just after seven, she saw Mitch asleep in his bed and had no idea when he'd come in.

Standing, looking at the hotel parking lot, Kendra was grateful for the fact that she had a task to accomplish, something to set her mind apart from worrying that her friendship with Mitch might be falling apart. They had never gotten in a fight. Ever. And all it had taken was one day on the road for tempers to rise. Was this the beginning of the end for them?

Immediately after getting up, Kendra had begun researching local towing companies, to finally put the issue of the dead Mustang to rest. It wouldn't be complicated. All she needed to do was get towed to the nearest gas station, where she could fill up and be on her way.

What sounded like a simple plan was complicated by only one thing: this was going to cost a *lot*. And Kendra knew she couldn't go to a local ATM or use her credit card to pay for the tow truck. She also knew she couldn't call her parents to use their AAA account, which would either decrease the cost or erase the cost entirely.

So she had called a few places, hoping to find an affordable place that also seemed like it was run by people who wouldn't steal the classic car and ride off into the desert with it. The company she had gone with, Lamar & Sons, was her last, best hope.

But they were late.

Kendra paced nervously in front of the entrance doors to the hotel. She had called the business a few times asking for an updated time of arrival, but they had said the same thing every time: "He's on his way, miss. Not to worry."

Kendra had never been comforted by someone telling her "not to worry." Usually, in fact, it had the opposite effect.

– – –

Upstairs in the dark, stuffy bedroom, Mitch was only half awake and reliving the night before. He had come home at 3 a.m. to find Kendra fast asleep. And since he hadn't gotten any *where are you?* texts from her, he assumed she had been asleep a long time. He'd slipped into bed and fell asleep within seconds.

He wasn't ready to open his eyes yet. He could tell that when he did, searing pain would rocket throughout his skull. And besides, keeping his eyes closed meant he could happily keep reliving the night before.

The night was still when he stepped out of the hotel doors, headed to the In-N-Out across the street. There were no stars in the sky, but there was an easy, lofty breeze in the air that invigorated his every step. It felt good to get outside the room and put the bad blood that had mysteriously risen between him and Kendra on the back burner for a while.

He tore open the white, red, and yellow-colored In-N-Out bag like a kid on Christmas morning. A gluttonous feast of grease and salt was exactly what he needed. In-N-Out Burger had been Mitch's happy place for as long as he could remember. It was a California chain, but there were two in Salt Lake—much to the dismay of Mr. and Mrs. Matlin. After classic romance movies, In-N-Out was Mitch's next greatest passion. He had only been allowed one trip a month growing up. Mitch could have hardly imagined a more perfect thing on his first night of true adulthood: eating at an In-N-Out mere feet from the Vegas Strip. There was *nothing* his parents would like about this situation.

Midway through his meal—a double cheeseburger with everything on it and an order of In-N-Out's classic "Animal Style" fries, covered in onions and cheese and secret sauce—he felt his phone vibrate in his pocket. Thanks to his greasy, damp fingers, Mitch left a thick streak on the screen of his phone when he swiped to unlock it.

The text was from Patrice.

Mitch nearly spit out the mouthful of burger he was working on. Hanging on every word, he read the text.

Hey cutie, where you at? The MGM was dead, we're just chillin on the strip now. Gonna get some ice cream. Keep things PG ;)

He read the text maybe twenty times in quick succession, salivating over a few individual things— "cutie," "chillin," the winky face—and relishing the entire situation. A totally hot girl in her twenties was giving him an open invitation. *What?!*

He suddenly had no appetite, even though he had eaten less than half of what was in front of him. How was he supposed to respond?

He weighed his options. *What do I tell Kendra?* he wondered, picturing his friend sitting alone upstairs. *She seems unhappy already . . . She'll be furious if I leave* her behind for the entire night. *This was supposed to be our trip, not just mine—and definitely not Patrice's!*

Maybe I can invite Kendra along, he realized. But quickly, that thought faded. *Patrice only gave her number to me, not both of us. And she didn't say anything about Kendra in the text.*

Normally, Mitch included Kendra in everything— from trips to the grocery store, to asking people to prom. But this was different. It was his moment. Not Kendra's.

After a minute of thinking, the decision was obvious. He had to say yes. For all he knew, this opportunity would happen only once. Turning Patrice down could result in complete and total rejection for the rest of the trip. If he pitched it to Kendra that way, she would get it . . . right?

With that, Mitch crafted a text back to Patrice. *It has to be simple,* Mitch said to himself, *but enthusiastic—but not too enthusiastic!* After a few minutes' work, he sent:

For sure, I'm over at the hotel but I can meet you guys in a few. Drop me a pin?

And twenty minutes later, Mitch was walking briskly up the Strip itself. The outrageous buildings, lit to make them even more imposing and glorious than they already were, felt like the perfect backdrop to what he was about to do. The speakers perched in the trees along the sidewalk pumped bass-heavy dance music, the perfect underscore for the epic night Mitch was about to have.

He fought off the impulse to pump his fist in the air like Rocky racing up the steps of the Philadelphia Museum of Art. But just barely.

Mitch knew he was coming up on the meeting place Patrice had given him: the BLVD Creamery, just south of the Mandarin Oriental. And now, as he swerved around slow-moving tourists along the Strip, the sky-scraping hotel, its towers folded together like a paper fan, rose in front of him.

He slowed his pace to a stroll, catching his breath.

The last thing he wanted to do was show up in any way other than totally cool. If he had learned one thing from being turned down by Nora Dickinson, it was this: don't try. If you want it, you won't get it.

These were the words ricocheting through Mitch Matlin's head as he spotted Patrice and Abby seated at a little table outside the ice cream shop. He took a deep breath, and called, "Patrice! Abby!"

They turned their heads—glamorously, their hair tumbling off of their shoulders like the sexiest waterfall Mitch had ever seen—to meet his eyes with their own. They smiled softly, and Mitch tried to do the same— *Keep it cool, Matlin!* he scolded himself—as he walked across the shop.

"Took you long enough," Patrice said as she stood up to greet him. Mitch stumbled over his words and managed to get out "Sorry, it was—" before she had her arms around him, giving him a firm but chaste hug hello. It was more than enough time, however, for Mitch to be knocked almost unconscious by her scent, like sandalwood.

She pulled away, sitting back down at the table. "We ordered a sundae, but we can't finish it," Patrice said, smiling. "Hope you can help us out."

She could even make that simple question a turn-on! Mitch's heart fluttered. He wasn't sure he could handle spending time in these girls' presence. It might just kill him.

Patrice pushed the sundae toward him, and Mitch immediately regretted his earlier decisions. There were still multiple scoops of chocolate and strawberry ice cream left, as well as heaps of whipped cream and pools of hot fudge. *Why did I make myself finish all of that In-N-Out?* he scolded himself. *If I eat more than three bites of ice cream, I'll probably vomit all over them. Good work, stupid!*

"I can totally help you out," Mitch said casually.

Abby piped up, smiling at Mitch with a little evil glint in her eye. "Good, that's the only reason we called you anyway."

"Definitely," Patrice said. "The only reason." She reached across the table and put her hand on top of

Mitch's. If his hand wasn't occupied, he would have pinched himself.

Mitch did noble work on the sundae, though couldn't quite polish it off. "I'll let this slide. This time," Patrice said, winking.

Then, quickly, they were off on the next adventure. Patrice and Abby had a plan, and they insisted Mitch tag along.

The plan took the trio walking up the Strip even farther, across busy Harmon Avenue, past the imposing Cosmopolitan hotel. Mitch knew where they were headed even before Patrice pointed to it: The Fountains of Bellagio.

He didn't say it out loud, to avoid sounding like a little kid on vacation, but this had been what he most wanted to see in Las Vegas. The Fountains were iconic, internationally recognizable for their grandeur and intoxicating beauty.

And they did not disappoint in real life, either. As the trio approached the fountains, they were midway through a long sequence, set to Frank Sinatra songs.

The jets of water, illuminated from all directions in shades of gold, red, and blue, shot impossibly high into the air, spinning off diagonally and dovetailing with others . . . They looked almost human in how they bent and danced in the air.

"I think they're so sexy," Patrice said softly as they admired the spectacle. All Mitch could do was nod. He looked over at Patrice and they made eye contact, holding each other's gaze for what felt like ages. It was all too perfect: the gorgeous beacon of Las Vegas was spinning through the air, reflected in the eyes of one of the most beautiful women Mitch had ever seen, and Frank Sinatra—the embodiment of Las Vegas—crooned about love and life in the background.

Mitch realized, looking into Patrice's eyes, that he hadn't asked any questions since meeting up with her and Abby. He was perfectly willing to follow their lead, all too happy to be their boy toy for the evening.

Then, somehow, he was alone with Patrice—and they were definitely not in front of the Fountains of Bellagio anymore. They were leaning up against the red Mustang back in the parking lot of the hotel, their bodies pulled close and their lips pressed hard together, dancing and weaving together like they were trying to pin each other down.

He had no idea how he'd gotten there, which was strange given that he hadn't drunk any alcohol or ingested any other kind of substance . . . but despite everything, Mitch was certain that this was the happiest moment of his life.

Once Mitch replayed this entire sequence five times in a row in his head, he finally opened his eyes. A wave of searing pain crushed his skull, almost forcing his eyelids back together. Rolling over to the other side of the bed, twisting in agony, Mitch's stomach roiled and he felt hot acid bubbling up his esophagus.

Why do I feel so terrible? Mitch wondered. Had he accidentally gotten drunk? On what? He'd seen representations of hangovers and blackouts in movies and on TV, and this was nothing like that. It was truly frightening to have such a gaping hole in your memory. Especially if you had no idea how it could have possibly happened.

Mitch rolled on the bed, twisting himself up in the sheets. He'd never felt sicker in his whole life. *What if I die right here in this bed?*

As he contemplated that question, the memory of kissing Patrice fell back over him like a warm summer rain, soothing every ache and twinge of nausea. He could still feel her chest pushed hard up against his, her long luscious fingers searching and kneading the muscles of his upper back.

Maybe dying here in this bed would be worth it, he mused, before tumbling back into a heavy slumber.

– – –

Outside in the parking lot, Kendra was beyond irritated. The day was getting much hotter, fast. Her scalp was frying like a piece of bread left too long in the toaster.

After six total calls to Lamar & Sons, Kendra had

still only heard one response: "Not to worry." She had spent the forty-five minutes waiting outside composing the first thing she'd say to the tow truck driver, if and when he finally showed up.

"You expect me to pay for this, you jerk?!"

Or, "What, did you need a tow truck for your tow truck?"

Or, "Who's out of gas: me, or you?"

Those last two are pretty similar, Kendra admitted to herself. *I'll figure it out in the moment.*

After she could pace no more in front of the hotel doors, Kendra walked over to the Mustang, parked in a lonely corner of the lot. It still *looked* perfect, at least. The paint job was immaculate, shimmering in the brutal sunshine.

Kendra was overcome with guilt, for the umpteenth time that morning. What would her dad say if he could see her now? *Probably nothing,* Kendra thought. *He'd be too furious and disappointed for words.*

Her dad had done the most generous and trusting thing she could remember him ever doing: he gave her something he loved. He had given her a piece of himself. He had worked on this car—preserved it, perfected it—and, if he didn't love Kendra so much and want to see her happy, would have been thrilled to keep it inside, polished and immaculate.

And what had Kendra done with that trust? She'd cast it aside like a toy she'd gotten bored with. *He was right to be nervous,* Kendra thought. *I'm still a kid. I can't be trusted.*

Suddenly, Kendra was snapped out of her miserable reverie. She noticed something sticking out from under the Mustang, lying flat on the pavement behind the back right tire. It was brown and wrinkly. At first glance, Kendra thought it was a snake and jumped back. But when it didn't move, she approached it again, leaning down to get a closer look. It was a brown leather belt.

Weird, Kendra thought dryly. She stood back up and looked around the parking lot. *There aren't any cars nearby . . . where would this have come from? Unless . . .*

Her heart pounding, Kendra leaned down again,

getting flat on the pavement. She looked under the car, her eyes searching for . . . *What, exactly? A dead body?*

But there was nothing there. Just the lonely belt, cast asunder by some unknown someone, for some unknown reason. Before Kendra could wonder too long about where the belt came from, the rumble of a tow truck rose up behind her and she turned to face it, preparing to unleash her rage on the unprofessional fool who'd kept her waiting for so long.

"G'morning, sunshine!" came the cheerful, gruff call from the truck's cab. The skinny, suntanned, heavily tattooed arm of the driver stuck out of the window and waved at her as he pulled the tow truck up beside the Mustang.

Kendra squinted up at the driver, her blood pulsing. It was bad enough having to wait in the brutal morning sunshine. Now she was being catcalled to boot.

The driver put the truck in park and hopped out. "Hey, why don't you give me a smile?" he said, walking over to Kendra. "Sun's out! It's another beautiful day in the desert!"

"Well, my car's dead," Kendra said flatly. "I'll give you a smile once it's up and running again, thank you very much."

"Understood," the man said, extending his hand. "Name's Lamar by the way." Kendra took his hand and shook it firmly. It was so calloused and tough that if she had been blindfolded, she might have thought he was wearing a battered old suede work glove.

"Kendra," she said curtly. "So, you own the business? Lamar & Sons?" Lamar just blinked vaguely, looking back at her. "Or maybe you're Lamar Jr.?"

"Last name's Lamar, actually," he said. "Total coincidence." He stared at her again blankly, as if waiting for her to continue the conversation. But before Kendra could pipe in, he threw his head back and cackled. "Gotcha! Yes, I'm Lamar. I started the business. But I don't have any sons. Just thought that sounded like a more legit business, you understand."

Kendra was in no mood to laugh. After a few seconds, Lamar seemed to get the memo. "So anyway, what do we have here, hon?"

"Oh, uh . . . " Kendra started, so thrown off by the bad jokes that she had forgotten why this strange man was even here next to her. "So this is my dad's 1970 Mustang here—"

"Well I can see that!" Lamar exploded cheerfully. "You're telling me about what kinda car this is, as if I haven't wanted one of these babies my whole dang life!"

Oh no, Kendra thought, a pit opening up in her stomach. *He's going to steal this thing right out from under my nose.*

She tried to relax the situation. "Well, yes. It's a very pretty car."

"So what'd you do to her?" Lamar demanded. "Nothing permanent, I hope."

"I hope not, too," Kendra said. "It . . . ran out of gas." She could feel her cheeks flushing as Lamar gawked at her, obviously shocked at her irresponsibility. Then he threw back his head and laughed again.

"You must be yankin' my chain, little lady!" He

slapped the side of the Mustang giddily. "You got a good sense'a humor on you, I'll tell you what!"

"Not joking," Kendra said, her temper flaring. "I know it was really stupid, and trust me, I'm mad enough at myself without you making fun of me."

Lamar stopped laughing immediately and blinked at her. "Understood. Well, I should ask, the engine been worked on at all? Any tweaks, upgrades, anything like that?"

Kendra cursed herself for not knowing for sure, but said the only thing she could think of. "Well, it's been in a garage for at least twenty years. I don't think it has too many miles on it."

"What does the odometer say?" Lamar asked, approaching the driver's side door. Peeking in the window he declared, "My goodness, only a thousand! Practically an infant!"

"Is that a good thing?" Kendra asked suspiciously.

"You bet," Lamar said. "Now, you have a choice. Because I'll be honest with you, you didn't need to call me at all."

"What?!" Kendra bellowed. "What do you mean?"

Lamar seemed confused. "Don't you know? You can buy cans of gasoline. Won't cost you more than ten or twenty bucks, I should think. You got no other problems that I can see. If you get yourself to a gas station, you can buy gasoline right there and won't have to move the car an inch."

Kendra's knees buckled and she practically sank to the pavement. "I feel like such an idiot," she said. In the blink of an eye, she felt like a foolish young kid, too ignorant of the ways of the world to be out here alone.

Lamar continued without any note of comfort in his voice. "I'll drive you to a gas station. There are a few right nearby. On the house."

Kendra tapped her foot anxiously as she considered Lamar's proposition. *It would be nice to save money,* she thought. *But do I really want to climb into a truck with this crusty old guy?*

As she thought about it, Kendra couldn't help but picture what Mitch was doing just then. He was probably just snoozing away in the room, having the most relaxing vacation of his life, rather than the adventurous one they'd planned. She assumed that if he'd woken up he would have texted her by now, but who knew? Maybe he was just texting with that girl he was all gaga for. Maybe he'd left his best friend in the dust for good.

"I'll take you up on that free ride," she said confidently. "Thank you." Lamar tipped an invisible cap, smiled, and climbed into the truck.

Hey bud, she texted Mitch. Getting a ride to a gas station now in a tow truck (long story). The truck is from Lamar & Sons. The license plate number is Nevada LJH119. Not sure where the gas station is yet, but I'll let you know. She hit SEND and then realized she should clarify.

This is in case I get abducted or murdered or something ;)

Kendra climbed into the passenger side of the truck and buckled the seatbelt.

"Nearest station is the Shell farther down on Tropicana. At Rainbow, I believe," Lamar said. "Just a few minutes."

She quickly texted Mitch. *It's the Shell station on Tropicana and Rainbow Boulevard.*

Then her eyes caught something lying on the ground between the seats: a sawed-off double-barrel shotgun. Her eyes nearly exploded out of her skull.

Without even looking over at her, Lamar spoke up. "Don't worry, hon. That's only for emergencies."

– – –

Mitch's eyes flew open again to three shrill dings on his phone. He hauled himself out from under the covers and moved across the room. Coming to the pile of clothing surrounding his wide-open suitcase, he dug through his discarded shirt and pants to find where he had buried his phone. As he picked up his jeans to search the pockets, he realized his belt was nowhere to be seen. He cursed himself for owning only one belt. The thought of continually hiking up his pants for the rest of this trip made his headache even worse than it already was.

Finally, he dug out his phone and looked at the screen, to find three texts from Kendra. He almost did a double take. Why hadn't she woken him up earlier when she went to deal with this? Why did she have to leave him on his own?

What is this power play? Mitch wondered. Kendra had been acting so bitter and strange the night before, and it looked like the morning hadn't calmed her nerves at all. She was probably going to be all snide about the fact that he didn't help out with the car, when she hadn't even given him a chance to help!

He looked at the texts blankly, unsure of how to respond or what to do. He could be the bigger person and find a way over to the gas station to meet her there. Or he could say he would have helped if she had let him help, which was true! *But do I really want to keep this animosity going back and forth?* he wondered.

His mental back-and-forth was interrupted by his phone springing to life and vibrating in his hand. Patrice was calling.

"Hello?" he asked sleepily, holding the phone up to his ear.

"Hey, stranger," came her sultry voice from the other end of the line. She sounded just like she had the night before, as if the lack of sleep had no effect on her at all. "What are you up to?"

Mitch's heart skipped a beat. *Whoa,* he thought. *She can't get enough!*

"Um, well . . . I just woke up, actually," he said. "I feel like garbage."

Patrice giggled slyly. "From what? The ice cream? Or were you partying too hard before you found us?"

Mitch blushed. "Yeah, I guess from that ice cream. You guys really did me in." *Such a sexy conversation topic,* Mitch thought sarcastically. *You should always talk about how bloated you are, that really wins girls over.*

"So, what are you up to today?" *A little pushy,* Mitch thought. *But that's just how into me she is, I guess!*

"Well, I actually just got a text from Kendra. She's out dealing with our stupid car that died," he said.

"It's not stupid!" Patrice giggled. "It's what brought us together, after all."

Mitch smiled, feeling like he had died and gone to heaven all over again. "That's true. That old red Mustang." Without meaning to, Mitch's mind flashed on an image of him and Patrice sitting next to each other in the well-appointed living room of their home in the suburbs. They were wearing thick wool sweaters and talking to their children about "that old red Mustang" that brought them together. Their kids smiled up at them, charmed by their parents' love for each other. Mitch put his arm around his lovely wife and she snuggled in. The fireplace roared . . .

"So, you're at the hotel?" Patrice asked, bringing Mitch back to the present.

"Yep," Mitch said. "Still wearing my pajamas and everything." He was getting pretty good at this sly come-on thing!

"Pajamas sound pretty comfy," Patrice said. He could hear her smiling warmly on the other end of the line.

But a voice crept into Mitch's head, reminding him that Kendra was out at a gas station taking care of a major mistake *both* of them had made. He would officially be a bad friend if he knowingly ignored her text and met up with Patrice instead.

As if she could hear him wrestling with the situation, Patrice said, "I can be there in five minutes. That sound good?"

– – –

The Shell station looked functional, but there wasn't anyone around. There weren't any cars filling up at the eight pumps, no cars parked in front of the convenience store, and, though Kendra searched the store's windows for signs of life, no one there either. *So close and yet so far,* Kendra thought. Her mind hadn't ventured far from the shotgun sitting between the seats. Why would he ever need that thing? Was the desert really crawling with people that dangerous?

"Where's the welcome wagon?" Lamar said quietly as the truck pulled into the empty parking lot.

"Ha," Kendra laughed tensely. "Looks like no one got the memo." She spied a sign on the door of the small convenience store that read, *Back at 12:30!*

Lamar put the truck in park. "I'm sorry to say, I'm not gonna be able to wait with you here. I got another pickup in half an hour and traffic on the interstate looks bad."

Kendra nodded, her mind quickly becoming saturated with the different problems staring her in the face all at once. "I can call an Uber, I guess," she said. "After I buy the gas."

"A what?" Lamar asked.

Kendra shook her head, forcing a smile. "Never mind."

"Alright, then," Lamar said. "I'll be on my way. You be safe out here."

Kendra stuck out her right hand like a high-powered CEO at the end of a board meeting. Lamar took it uneasily, but gave her a firm shake. "Thanks again for your charity, my man. I'll give you five stars on Yelp. No, I'll convince Yelp to let me give you *six* stars!"

"Don't know what that is," Lamar said. "Anyway, stay out of the sun. Overheating makes you crazy." Kendra gave Lamar one final smile as she got out of his truck. He pulled back out onto Tropicana and was gone.

Kendra moved under the overhang above the gas pumps where it was slightly cooler. She stood in the shade and rubbed her temples, trying to remain calm.

Kendra spent the first few minutes in the stifling heat constantly checking her phone. She wanted to check the time and see if Mitch would finally prove himself to be a halfway-decent friend. The time passed slowly, and Mitch didn't respond. Eventually Kendra put her phone in her pocket and closed her eyes. *I've never meditated before,* Kendra thought, *but this would be a pretty good time to find some inner peace.*

After what felt like hours of silence, a warm and luscious voice came up right behind her. "Hey," it said. Kendra spun around, wild-eyed, looking for the gas station attendant. He was finally there. "Over here!" came the voice again.

Kendra looked to her right to see Jack the Jackal leaning up against the gas pump just a few feet from where she stood. He smirked at her through his leering yellow eyes, his long mouth turned up in a creepy smile.

Chapter Six

"Jack?" Kendra asked softly. She pinched herself, convinced she must be dreaming. But Jack the Jackal went nowhere. Lamar's voice echoed in her head. *Overheating makes you crazy.*

"Take a picture, it'll last longer," Jack the Jackal said. He didn't talk like he did in the cartoon. When he spoke, he sounded like Frank Sinatra, his voice velvety and alluring. "Hello?" he asked again, standing up straight from the gas pump. "Cat got your tongue?"

Then Jack was directly in front of her again, that snide smile still spread out across his face. "Don't you remember me?" he said smoothly.

"Of course I remember you," Kendra said, somehow unable to resist talking to him. "You're back home in my room. You're sitting on my bed. And you're a *doll*. You don't talk."

"Well, see, that's where you're wrong," he said, an edge creeping into his voice. A small breeze blew across the flat expanse of the parking lot, causing a small puff of dust to lift off of his brown-gray fur. Now that she looked at him, Kendra realized, Jack the Jackal didn't look so good. He looked skinnier, and his fur was patchy.

"You used to watch cartoons every Saturday morning, Kendra. What happened to you? You must miss me so much. You must long for the days when you could sit down, eating a bowl of sugary cereal, and watch me chase that stupid bird all over the desert." He gestured toward the dusty expanse of the surrounding desert with a stick-like arm. "Admit it. You miss me."

"I grew up. I don't miss you," Kendra said, her eyes starting to droop from the heat and the intensity of his yellow eyes boring into hers. "I still have you—the doll, I mean—but that's it. I'm a different person now."

"Turn around and get out of here," Jack the Jackal said, walking slowly towards her. "Get back to where it's safe." His big dusty feet padded softly toward her, one after another. His smile grew more and more menacing with every step, revealing huge yellow teeth. *I don't remember him having teeth,* Kendra thought, her pulse rising. She wanted to turn and run, but her feet were fixed to the ground . . .

"I said *get out!*" He was inches away from her, his teeth shimmering in the sunlight . . .

"Kendra!" A male voice made Kendra's eyelids fly open. She looked around to find she had apparently sat down against a cement pillar. And had fallen asleep. She looked hurriedly around her to see if the jackal was calling her name, but he was nowhere to be seen.

Suddenly, a hand was on her shoulder and Kendra screamed, rolling away.

"Whoa, whoa!" Mitch stammered, his eyes

searching her; he looked almost scared of her. Kendra breathed hard, trying to shake herself out of her daze.

"Oh," Kendra said. "Mitch. It's you."

"Hey, are you okay?" Mitch asked cautiously. "Did you fall asleep out here?"

"I . . . I guess so," Kendra said. "The heat." She rubbed her eyes, her mind still focused on Jack the Jackal. The dream had seemed so vivid, like the desert was playing tricks on her. Or trying to tell her something.

Without looking at Mitch, Kendra whispered, "Where were you?"

"I know," he said, defeated. "I'm so sorry."

"Seriously," Kendra said. "*Where were you?*"

"I was asleep," Mitch said. He grimaced, looking completely pathetic.

"Until noon?" Kendra asked. Her temper was rising again. "What did you do last night?"

"It's a long story," Mitch said. "I'm sorry," Mitch said again.

"Supposedly the guy will be back in a few minutes,"

Kendra said bitterly. "Once we buy a can of gas, we can go." Mitch nodded heavily. They sat down side by side on the asphalt under the overhang.

"You know," Kendra said, suddenly sharp, "I should still be mad at you." Rather than focusing on the mystery of her own mind, she wanted answers from Mitch.

"Oh, I know," Mitch said. "I'm mad at myself."

"*Now* will you tell me what you did last night?"

– – –

Eventually the attendant returned, and Mitch paid for the can of gas. During the Uber drive back to the hotel parking lot, Mitch spilled: the journey to find Patrice and Abby; the wandering around the Strip; and the last thing he remembered, which was, as he said, a "single, solitary kiss goodnight with Patrice." He wasn't quite ready to divulge every detail, and he definitely didn't want to open the can of worms that involved him inexplicably losing his memory for a few hours.

"You smooched her?!" Kendra exploded.

"Shh!" Mitch said, looking awkwardly at the driver of the car. "I think so," he whispered. "But like I said, my memory is totally fuzzy."

"You little turd," Kendra said. "Are you kidding me?"

"Are you mad?" he asked.

"No, I'm just kind of nauseous," she said. "Is she like a cradle robber or something?"

Before he could respond, the Uber pulled into the hotel parking lot, and he and Kendra got out. As they walked to the Mustang and Kendra began the process of refilling the tank, Mitch said, "Well, I don't want to meet up with her again. Honestly. She's been texting me again today. It's kinda weirding me out."

"Yeah, dude, me too," Kendra said. "Let's avoid her, huh?" She unscrewed the cap on the gas tank and tipped the nozzle of the gas can inside. Both she and Mitch were silent as the gas tank refilled. Once the can was empty, Kendra moved around to the driver's side door and opened it.

"Here goes nothing," she muttered tensely as she

put the key in the ignition. The engine revved twice and then quickly turned over, humming again. Kendra pumped her fists in the air and cheered. "Yes!" she yelled. "Relief!" Mitch banged his palm on the trunk in celebration. Kendra raced back to where Mitch was standing and hugged him.

"Thank God," she said. They breathed two big sighs of relief and then pulled apart.

"I'm so sorry about everything," he said. "The gas tank, last night, this morning. I have a lot to make up for. I totally get why you're mad."

Kendra nodded. "I feel pretty weird that you just left me in the hotel and didn't invite me. Not cool."

"I know," Mitch said. She was completely right.

"But on the other hand, we weren't really getting along all that well last night."

"Also correct," Mitch said. "Did I do something wrong?"

"I don't even remember," Kendra said. "I was mad at you about the car, but I was also really mad at myself. I just wasn't sure I wanted to be here. If any of that struggle and frustration had been worth it."

Mitch paused, wondering where this was leading.

"But after some thinking," Kendra said, "I want to give Vegas another day."

Mitch nodded, relieved. "I'm really happy to hear that," he said. "Let me make last night up to you. I was a really terrible friend last night and this morning. I'm really sorry."

Kendra patted his hand. "It's okay, my son. Just don't ditch me because some pretty girl tells you she wants to hang out."

"Deal!" Mitch cheered.

"Oh, right," Kendra said, a smile creeping across her face, "there's one more thing." Mitch watched tensely as Kendra bent down and picked something up off the ground. It was brown and more than a foot long, and for a terrifying second Mitch thought Kendra was handling a rattlesnake. But quickly he realized it was something else, and he felt his cheeks flush crimson.

He stuck out his hand and Kendra gave him his withered brown belt.

Kendra laughed. "Pants hanging a little loose today, Casanova?"

Chapter Seven

"Alright, let's see," Mitch said, looking towards the changing room door.

"Ugh, I don't know," Kendra groaned from inside.

"Come on!" Mitch cheered. "This one's the winner, I can feel it." Kendra opened the changing room door and stepped out gingerly, slowly revealing the outfit she was trying on: a long 1920s gold-sequined flapper girl dress, complete with a black feather boa, a feather in her hair, and long suede black gloves. In her hands she clasped a comically long cigarette holder.

"Oh yeah!" Mitch cheered. "I bet a bunch of kids tried to pull off this look at prom."

Kendra laughed too. "But nobody did it like me!"

"Excuse me!" came the voice of the prissy hipster girl working the floor of the vintage store. "Can you keep your voices down, please?"

"But she looks so good!" Mitch yowled.

Though the morning had been awful, Mitch and Kendra had forced themselves to make the rest of the day into the raucous Vegas adventure they really wanted. After laying low at the hotel and a quick trip to a diner for pancakes, Mitch and Kendra had jumped into the Mustang and headed out shopping. Tonight they would finally hit the Strip and make a killing at the casinos—and if they were going to do that, they needed to make a statement.

Before long, a picture of Kendra modeling the dress was up on Instagram. And immediately, the comments started rolling in:

Omg DYING!!

Mom <3

Watch out for all the crusty old men at the

casinos—they'll think you're the hottest thing they've seen since 1925!

Before long, Mitch had found an outfit for himself: a tuxedo jacket covered in garish 1970s floral print. Every color on the spectrum clashed and fought for space—so much so that if you looked at it long enough, you might go cross-eyed. Mitch paired the jacket with loose-fitting white linen pants and bright red deck shoes.

"You're one red nose away from the circus, bro," Kendra said, giggling. "And not like a nice clown, either. Like, the clown from *It*. You ever see that movie? He lures kids into the sewer and murders them. That's you, baby!" They doubled over in laughter as Mitch mimed stabbing Kendra with a machete and she died violently on the floor.

"Excuse me!" called the hipster girl again. "Are you two going to buy anything? Or are you just entertaining yourselves? Because I could be on my lunch break right now."

"Oh, we're buying!" Kendra called. "No price is too high for me!" She gestured to her outrageous neon-blue outfit. "I'm a Scandalous 1920s Girl! Look how much ankle I'm showing!"

"And I," Mitch said, "am the Least Successful Adult Film Star Ever."

While Mitch was shelling out the cash for the outfits, Kendra couldn't help but let her mind wander. *Remember me?* Jack the Jackal had asked, sneering at her. *It hasn't been that long, after all . . .*

Her heart rate quickened, thousands of thoughts echoing inside her skull all at once: Was something wrong with her brain? Did she have some sort of stroke or seizure out there? Was it some kind of sign, some kind of apparition that appeared only to her? Or was it just a dream?

"Kendra?" came Mitch's voice, as if from down a long hallway. "Kendra?" it came again, this time much clearer.

Kendra blinked back at Mitch, returning to the

room for the first time in what felt like hours. "Yeah?" she asked, trying to play it cool.

"Ready to go?" Mitch asked.

Kendra shook her head, trying to erase the questions booming inside her head. "Yep." This night was in the palm of their hands. The last thing Kendra wanted to do was ruin it with some kind of existential freak-out.

As Mitch and Kendra left the vintage shop, holding their outfits in multiple bulging canvas bags, Mitch's phone buzzed. He pulled it out to see a notification from Instagram. Kendra noticed his sharp intake of breath.

"What? What is it?" she asked, her voice edgy.

"Guess who just commented on that photo," Mitch said, smirking.

"Who?"

Mitch handed her the phone. And there was the comment, in all its glory. Kendra's heart warmed, and she suddenly felt like she could run the world. Adam Green—alone back in Salt Lake, twiddling his thumbs after what was probably an underwhelming prom with someone else—had commented just one, beautiful word: Jealous!

Kendra threw her head back to the sky, her mouth wide open, her arms flung wide like a medieval warrior who has just slayed an entire army with one hand. "*Victory! Is! Mine!*"

– – –

When their feet touched the sidewalk on Las Vegas Boulevard—which was not made of asphalt, but rather of fake marble tiling—Kendra and Mitch grabbed hands. They paused where they were, in front of the New York-New York hotel, with the shudders and clangs of the roller coaster overhead, and looked at each other, the lights of the Strip dancing in their eyes and over their outrageous, giddy outfits.

"Finally," Kendra said.

"Finally," Mitch replied. A moment passed between them—the kind of moment you almost never experience, when every good feeling you've ever had is compressed together in one perfect, almost uncontrollable ball of bright, boundless energy that burns in your chest. Mitch and Kendra were at a loss for words.

Eventually, Kendra found her words again and smiled slyly. "Wanna go on this stupid rollercoaster?" she asked. Mitch nodded frantically.

As the sun set west of the Strip, Mitch and Kendra sat in the front car of the roller coaster, steadily climbing up the first incline. The track rattled as the car was pulled upward into the wispy, salmon-colored clouds. At the crest of the hill, during the two seconds it took for the rest of the cars to climb up behind theirs, Kendra and Mitch took in the view. The craggy slopes of desert mountains lay far out ahead of them, darkening by the second. Roaring highways and thoroughfares, packed with cars swarming like a wasp's nest, spread out at the foot of the track. It was at once a gorgeous and hideous vista, natural wonders overlaid with man-made, metallic chaos.

Then suddenly, the coaster barreled downward, rocketing down its track. They screamed harder and louder than they ever had in their lives, nearly out of their minds with joy. The coaster flew up, down, and around—turning sideways to bend around a portion of the track, going completely upside down at others. It veered back toward the Strip, and as they were turning upside down in a loop-de-loop, the luscious emerald-green MGM Grand casino appeared to the right, majestic as the lights sprung up around and inside of it, like a hulking mass of sea glass. But then it was gone again, as the coaster tumbled onward, and Mitch and Kendra's screams echoed into the oncoming desert night.

Just two minutes later, Kendra and Mitch were walking ever so slowly through the roller coaster's exit, back onto Las Vegas Boulevard. "Wowee zowee," Mitch said, rubbing his temples. "That really wrecked me."

"Me too, yo," Kendra said, but she refused to be derailed. "Where to now? The American Dream?" She giggled.

"I say we hit up a casino," Mitch said. "No time like the present."

They looked across the street from where they stood at the hulking MGM Grand, its name in bold yellow shouting into the night. Without saying anything, Mitch looked back at Kendra, an eyebrow raised.

They didn't say much to one another as they approached the entrance of the casino. This would be the first test of their fake IDs. Kendra's stomach was tied in knots as they walked toward the door, her head filled with images of her showing up to Austin Lovelace's front door after paying thousands of dollars in fines or spending months in jail, demanding retribution. *You stupid piece of trash!* she'd shout, punching his dumb face with all her might. *Were you* trying *to do damage to my permanent record? What if I want to run for public office someday? Huh?! What do you have to say to that, Daddy?!*

Kendra willed herself to put the images out of her mind in the last few steps up to the doors of the MGM

Grand. The sliding doors gleamed ahead of them, and they fell in with the masses.

"Here we go!" Mitch whispered to her as the doors parted, and they entered the casino. All at once, they were hit by a blast of frigid air and the slaphappy melody of a new Carly Rae Jepsen single. Hordes of people milled around ahead of them—people of all shapes and sizes, wearing all kinds of clothing. Some people were as decked out as Mitch and Kendra were, including one person, who could have been any and all genders, wearing a dark red dress with a long train tripping along the ground behind them. But many of the sunburnt and starry-eyed people around them were not dressed to impress; instead they were wearing ratty polos and bedazzled Kiss T-shirts, baggy cargo shorts, and perilously tight miniskirts that didn't match.

Mitch gaped at the gamblers, who all seemed eons older than him and Kendra, and their fashion choices. "Maybe we're making *too much* of a statement?" Mitch asked, with real worry in his voice.

Kendra laughed sardonically. "They just need to get on our level," she said.

The inside of the casino was grander and more outrageous than they could have ever imagined. Gleaming fake stone columns and arches expanded upward and outward through the cavernous space. Everything seemed coated in a thick layer of gold. The luxurious decor clashed violently with the poppy music.

"This is . . . a lot," Mitch said. Kendra nodded slowly, completely overcome.

"We just have to find out how we buy chips," Kendra said. "That's what we're here to do. Let's make some money!" She shouted the last bit, pumping her fist in the air, demanding to be noticed. A bleary-eyed, middle-aged couple looked over at her in confusion.

"Seriously," Mitch said, already weary, "let's try to keep a *slightly* low profile for a while? At least until after we have to show our IDs?"

Kendra's giddy smile dropped away. "Oh," she said, "sure. You're right."

They passed a craps table where an old woman sat

alone. Kendra wondered whether the woman had been there since the casino first opened; in the dim light it was hard to tell where her beige cotton pants ended and the plush beige chair began. They passed a gleaming video poker station that prattled on, music and lights blaring, unattended.

They turned right past the first few tables and then saw it: the belly of the beast. A gaping, seemingly endless hall opened up ahead of them. There were thousands of frantic, colorful screens. More of the same average-looking people, drinks in hand, milled about, all of them gleefully lost.

"Holy crap," Mitch said, his eyes wide.

"I feel like we just walked into a cartoon," Kendra said, immediately remembering her fever dream from earlier in the day. Again, she willed herself to not think about it.

"Let's agree on how much we're spending," Mitch said. "We can't spend everything. I have a hundred and fifty left—for the whole rest of the trip."

Kendra pulled out her wad of cash from her pocket. "Yeah, I only have two hundred."

"That means we shouldn't spend more than fifty or so, each. Deal?"

"Deal."

Mitch stroked his chin. "So, if I'm doing my math correctly, we'll each start with fifty . . . "

"We'll leave town with a thousand!" Kendra said, high fiving him. "Let's do this!"

– – –

Kendra and Mitch spent the next two hours flying higher than high. They played the cheap slots almost exclusively, to make their money last longer. It was outrageously addictive; seeing three red Xs flash across the screen only made you want to put more money in and try again. Mitch sat in front of one screen for almost half an hour, staring a hole into the brightly lit screen and robotically pushing more and more money into the slot.

Kendra tapped him on the shoulder. "Hey, champ," she said. "How you doin'?"

Mitch felt like he had been woken up from a deep sleep. "How long have I been sitting here?" he asked. He looked at Kendra and saw faint red Xs on her face.

"An hour? Two? Ten?" Kendra giggled. "Who knows! You a millionaire yet?"

Mitch winced. "Not exactly."

"So listen," Kendra said. "I want to play poker. I've played online before. I'm pretty bad, but I like the whole vibe. Want to come?"

Mitch shifted in the leather chair, to which the seat of his linen pants was stuck with sweat. "I dunno, I'm pretty chill here," he said.

"You sure?" Kendra asked. Mitch nodded. "Alright, I'll be at those tables right back there." She pointed to a section of the floor devoid of crazy flashing lights, where long pendant lights hung from the ceiling over broad felt-topped tables.

Mitch saluted her. He watched her walk away, and then turned back to the screen. He wondered how

Kendra seemed to be having such a perfectly blissful time. *Maybe this Vegas thing isn't for me,* he reflected. *I thought it was, but . . .*

But before he could continue his thought, a familiar voice came up behind him. "Hey, stranger. Where've you been all my life?"

Patrice placed a long, lithe hand on his shoulder and squeezed—a little too hard.

Chapter Eight

KENDRA MADE HER WAY TO A SMALL KIOSK BEHIND which a little old man sat perched on a stool. A huge box of chips sat in front of him. "Is this where I buy chips?" Kendra asked, so confident now she felt like she owned the entire MGM Grand. "Poker chips, not potato chips. But if you have those kinda chips too, I wouldn't be mad."

"Just poker chips, I'm afraid," the man said. Kendra shrugged and slid forty dollars toward him. He nodded silently and moved a stack of chips toward her. But he stopped short, eyeing her. "You have ID?" he asked.

Kendra's heart skipped a beat. "Uh . . . " she

stammered. The man raised an eyebrow. "You bet," she said, pulling it out of her purse. The man took it and eyed it skeptically. An eternity seemed to pass while he considered it. Kendra repeated her full name, her birthday, and her home address feverishly in her head.

After what felt like a week, he nodded and handed her ID back, along with the chips. Kendra smiled and sauntered away. She tried to kick her heels in the air, but stumbled. Frantically she tried to recover. "Carpet's broken right there," she announced awkwardly to the few people who saw her stumble. "Broken carpet. Just FYI."

Kendra found her way to a poker table where players were filtering in and sat down on one end. The other players, who were all middle-aged men in wrinkled khakis and T-shirts, eyed her costume skeptically. Kendra met their gaze with a smirk, and none of them said anything. Eventually the dealer muttered, "Alright, everybody, we're playing Hold 'Em. Let's keep the game moving as much as possible, huh? Big blind, small blind, ante up."

Kendra studied her competition. They were all balding and all sporting bushy mustaches. The bright lights hanging over the table exposed the wide-open pores in their skin, the broken blood vessels on the tips of their noses. *They're gonna try and take advantage of me, a silly young girl who has no idea how to play,* Kendra thought. *I'll show them!*

She didn't, exactly, "show them," as after just a few hands her stack of chips had dwindled down to half of what it was.

"Might want to slow down there, my young *compadre*," the meek old dealer muttered.

Kendra stood up gingerly from her chair and gathered her chips. When she turned around, she came face to face with someone she never expected to see again.

"Hey, stranger," Abby said, looking straight into Kendra's eyes with a smoldering strength. "Where've you been all my life?"

— — —

Mitch couldn't tell if he was thrilled to see Patrice or terrified of her. Before he could think—and he was thinking rather slowly—Mitch blurted, "How did you find me?"

Patrice laughed, velvety and low. "The universe keeps bringing us together, baby," she said. "Abby's here somewhere, too. I guess this town's not big enough for the two of us."

"Something like that," Mitch said. Alarm bells were going off in his head. She was everywhere, and she was aggressive.

Patrice pouted. "Aren't you happy to see me?"

"Listen, Patrice," Mitch said, looking anywhere but directly into her deep brown eyes. "I had a lot of fun with you guys last night. Like, a lot of fun." Mitch willed himself to not think about the most tempting parts of the evening, namely the way the evening ended. "But," he continued, "me and Kendra are sort of doing our own thing now. So maybe we'll catch up with you guys another night, but—"

Patrice grabbed Mitch's chin and swiveled his

head, forcing him to make eye contact. But despite grabbing him, she smiled just as sweetly as ever. "I hear you, boo," she said. "But Abby and I are leaving town tomorrow. So, there's no night but tonight. And besides, I thought you two came here to make memories? I'd say you and I have a few more memories to make. Wouldn't you?"

She bit her lip just a little. *I thought women only did that in movies*, Mitch thought. "Patrice, I . . . " But he trailed off, feeling his strength leave him in an instant. Mitch smiled dopily.

"There we go," Patrice said, patting him on the head. *Oh, man,* Mitch thought, *I know this is a bad idea. I made a promise to Kendra. I already was a bad friend to her once on this trip. If I strand her again, she might never forgive me.* But he couldn't help but look Patrice up and down. Somehow she looked even better than the night before.

Without thinking any more, Mitch said, "Sorry I didn't text you back earlier. Kendra and I were—"

"Don't worry about it," Patrice said calmly. "I

know, you're on vacation. I just . . . I didn't get enough of you last night, is all."

Mitch's mind exploded, his whole body tingled. He couldn't believe he had tried to ignore Patrice all day—was he crazy? This girl was the stuff dreams are made of!

"I didn't get enough of you, either," Mitch said, edging closer to her.

Patrice put her hands on Mitch's chest and gently pushed him away. "Not here," she said. "Let's find somewhere a little more discrete, huh?" She grabbed Mitch's hand and led him away.

– – –

"Oh . . . hey," Kendra managed, trying to focus on Abby's steely-blue eyes. "Long time, no see."

"Not really," Abby said dryly. "We only met last night." *Your friend could teach you a couple things about charm,* Kendra mused. "Cute outfit, by the way. Sexy in a sort of black-and-white-movie way."

"Thanks," Kendra managed awkwardly. "Well, nice talking to you." She turned to walk back towards a slot machine where she might be able to actually win some money.

"Wait a minute," Abby said softly, putting her hand on Kendra's shoulder. "I have a friend who wants to meet you."

Kendra's stomach did a backflip. Though she didn't want to admit it, these were magic words. She looked back at Abby and smiled. "You don't say?" she said slyly. "Who is he?"

"Really good friend of mine," Abby said. "If he and I hadn't been friends since we were kids, I'd totally be dating him now. He's a second-string tight end on the UNLV football team, and he's a history major."

Kendra practically drooled. "Tight ends are muscly," she managed.

Abby laughed. "Yeah, he doesn't disappoint on that front. Like I said, he's a catch. But it won't ever happen between us, so we sort of wingman each other."

"I get it," Kendra said. "Things would be a whole

lot simpler if Mitch and I could see each other that way."

"Yeah, so anyway," Abby said somewhat hurriedly, "I told him about you and he's curious. Want to come meet him?"

Mitch will be so mad at me, Kendra thought. *Just after we promised to make the rest of this trip about us and nobody else.* "I'm sorry, I . . . "

But her voice trailed off as her mind kept racing. *Then again,* she thought. *He got a night alone with somebody last night. Maybe I deserve to do that for myself.* Before she could rethink the situation again, Kendra took a deep breath and said, "Let's do it."

Abby smiled and forcefully grabbed her hand, wasting no time leading Kendra across the casino floor. She winked. "Good choice."

— — —

"Wait, I think if you close that, we might be locked

out—" Mitch said frantically as Patrice closed the metal door behind her.

"Exactly," she said. The sultry glare was gone from her face.

Mitch looked around at their surroundings. They had left the casino. The smell of wet garbage hung in the air and he could hear the traffic out on Las Vegas Boulevard.

"Come on, kid," Patrice scolded, her voice suddenly harsh. "Put the pieces together."

Mitch looked at her, his mind racing. He tried to calm himself down, remembering why Patrice led him out here. It was definitely secluded, that was for sure. Nobody was going to come out of that door and interrupt them.

"I think we're alone now . . . " Mitch crooned, putting his hands on Patrice's shoulders and leaning in for a kiss.

"Oh, gross," Patrice spat, pushing him away. Mitch's stomach turned sour.

"What?" he stammered, shocked. "You didn't think so last night. You're the best kisser I ever kissed!"

"In your dreams, dude," Patrice said sternly. "I only kissed you once, and even that was too much. Granted, I don't like going around kissing eighteen-year-olds, but you gotta do what you gotta do."

"Hey," Mitch said, "how do you explain my belt coming off, then?" He winked.

Patrice laughed. "You did that on your own. And you can bet I walked away right then and there." She shuddered.

Mitch's pulse rose. "Did you get me drunk last night? I barely remember anything after the Bellagio fountains!"

Patrice smiled wickedly. "You didn't see me or Abby eat any of that sundae, did you?"

Mitch stammered. "Wait, what?"

She grabbed his chin and squeezed, hard. Slowly, like she was talking to a young child, she said, "We. Laced. The. Ice. Cream." She shook her head and looked away, laughing bitterly.

Mitch felt nauseous all over again. They *drugged* him? With ice cream? "But wait," Mitch said, "you got me all messed up last night, and for nothing? I still have all the money in my wallet, and we have the keys to the Mustang."

Patrice glared at him. "We thought you'd have the keys on you, genius. You *were* the one driving when we first met you, remember? So, rather than take your money and wait on the keys, we decided to put it off a day. It's not like you were going anywhere, anyway." She winked at Mitch in the way that, yesterday, made his heart race. But today, it made his blood boil.

Suddenly, the door Mitch was leaning on opened, and two more familiar faces appeared: Abby and an anxious Kendra, who was trying to wedge her hand out of Abby's. As they crossed the threshold of the door, Abby scooted a brick into the doorjamb to hold it open.

"Hey," Abby said to Patrice, business-like.

"Whoa, Abby," Kendra said. "No, no, this is Mitch.

I thought you said you were bringing me to *your* friend. This is *my* friend."

"Kendra . . . " Mitch said darkly. The giddiness the casino had put into him was fading now. This was bad.

"So, here's what's gonna happen," Patrice said plainly. "You're going to give us the money in your pockets, and you're gonna give us the keys to that sweet ride."

Kendra's blood ran cold, her head clearing and flooding with adrenaline. *No,* she thought, *this can't be happening.*

Nobody said anything for quite a while, and Patrice tapped her foot testily. "Hello? Earth to children?"

"No," Kendra said.

Abby raised an eyebrow, smirking. "Oh, really?" she said. "Look, there's two ways this can work out. One: you give us what we're asking for, and we disappear from your lives, never to be seen again. Sure, you lose some money and you lose your car, but you're still young—you have your whole lives ahead of you! So, how bad is it, really?"

"Or," Patrice cut in, "the other option: we make things a lot more unpleasant for you." She slowly pulled something out from the pocket of the leather jacket she was wearing: A Swiss Army knife.

"Oh God," Mitch sputtered. His heart was frantically beating out of his chest.

"Yeah, 'oh God' is right," Abby said.

"So, come on, let's go," Patrice said.

Kendra—in spite of everything—laughed. She chuckled, and then she really laughed, throwing her head back and cackling up towards the starless blue-black sky.

"What?!" Patrice demanded. "What are you laughing about?"

"What's wrong with her?" Abby asked. "Is she having a stroke or something?"

"No, I just have a great sense of humor," Kendra said. "I'm just amused by this whole little situation here."

"I'm pointing a knife at you, little girl," Patrice spat. "I don't know what's so funny about that. I'm telling you, I'll use this if you don't hurry up. Seriously, those keys. Where are they?"

"Why are you doing this?" Mitch demanded. "What is wrong with you?"

Abby shrugged. "Las Vegas is swimming with easy marks like the two of you. People come, people go. We wait around and make the best of them."

"That's awful," Mitch said.

Patrice just laughed.

"Haven't exactly had great romantic rolls of the dice have we, Mitch?" Kendra said ruefully, looking over at him.

Matching her eyes made Mitch's head clear—at least a little bit. For the umpteenth time on this trip, he was endlessly thankful she was there. *And to think, I put our friendship on the brink because I thought this woman was in love with me,* he scolded himself.

"Yeah," he said. "Looks like our struggle wears on, friend-o."

"Very cute," Abby said. "But you can have your

heart-to-heart after we're gone. Come on, the money and the keys!"

Kendra did something that nearly made Mitch's head explode: she pulled her keys out of her pocket and slowly handed them over to Patrice. Then, silently, she pulled out the thin stack of bills left in her pocket. "Come on," she said softly to Mitch. "Give her your cash." Gritting his teeth, Mitch pulled out his wallet and handed over a stack of bills, the final hundred dollars he was saving for the drive home.

"So, she really *is* the smart one," Abby said sarcastically after Patrice had collected the money and the keys. "Mitch, you could learn something."

Mitch was too furious and terrified to offer a response. All he could do was stare at the knife Patrice was still holding.

"Well, it's been a pleasure," Patrice said. "Don't worry, kids, somebody'll love you. Honestly, Abby and I did enjoy our time with you. And now," she said, holding up the stolen goods, "we'll remember it fondly."

The women brushed past Kendra and opened the door back into the casino. After it slammed shut, Mitch and Kendra quickly hugged each other close, grateful beyond words that they had survived and found their way out of being held at knifepoint. They released each other and Kendra smiled at Mitch.

"You know, they're right. I *am* the smart one, and I have a plan."

– – –

Abby and Patrice leaned up against each other in the backseat of their Uber back to the hotel. The driver was blaring Justin Bieber with the windows down, and the warm summer evening breeze blew in the open windows. The only thing between them and that Mustang was some really bad traffic.

"Can't you go around?" Abby asked the driver impatiently.

The driver, slouched over the steering wheel, offered no response.

"Babe," Patrice said, patting Abby's leg, "there's no rush! We'll get there when we get there, and then we'll take off. Those kids can't do anything now. They're gonna cower in that alley for hours! Did you see how scared they were?" Patrice warped her face into a cartoon of fear and sadness, blubbering nonsense words.

Abby sighed like she was relaxing on a warm Caribbean beach. "I wish they were all this easy."

When the Uber pulled into the parking lot of the hotel twenty-five minutes later, both Patrice and Abby's hearts froze. There was the Mustang, right where they knew it'd be—but there was a tow truck next to it, its engine running. And the truck's driver, an older, no-nonsense man, was stepping out of the driver's side door.

"Evening!" he shouted to the car. Abby and Patrice got out of the Uber, but before the car could pull back out onto Tropicana, the truck driver spoke up.

"Hey, driver! Hold on a sec, will ya?" The Uber driver, snarling as he slouched over the steering wheel, nonetheless followed the truck driver's demand and stayed put.

"Who are you?" Patrice demanded. "This is our car."

"Well, I know for a fact that ain't true," the tow truck driver said. "Name's Lamar, by the way."

"I don't give a single—"

"Hey now," Lamar said. "I'm trying to be courteous here, why don't you do me the same, eh?"

"Look," Patrice said, pulling out the keys to the Mustang. "These are the keys. This is our car. You must be confused, old man."

He took a deep breath through his nose. Patrice was ready to scream. He seemed not at all terrified. What was wrong with him?

"I'm the furthest thing from confused, in point of fact," he said. "See, what I think is this: it's people like you that give Las Vegas a bad name."

Abby groaned, stamping her foot like a toddler.

"I mean it," Lamar continued. "This is a historic place, it's a beautiful place. But people come here and only want to rob people. They build huge, hulking buildings—*shrines*—to theft and greed. And tons of poor suckers find their way here, only to get burned just like the other poor souls who suffered before 'em." He took another deep breath through his nose, looking up at the sky. "When I was born, the Strip was smaller, and the lights were less powerful. We had stars then.

"But you know what keeps me here?" he continued, looking back down at Abby and Patrice. "Even though it's changed, it's still the desert, and it's still the Wild Wild West. So," he started, pulling out a sawed-off double-barreled shotgun from under his denim jacket, "you're gonna hand me those keys, those bills, and your little knife, and you're gonna take your high heels and scurry back from whence you came. Deal?"

Abby and Patrice stared back at him, their blood boiling. "Stick around any longer and I'll call the cops," Lamar said. But still they didn't move a muscle.

The Uber driver yelled from behind them. "Are you gonna need a ride somewhere else? Because I have somebody else I can go pick up! . . . Hello?"

Getting impatient, Lamar pulled back the hammer of the shotgun. Patrice's eyes opened wide, and she quickly tossed the keys in Lamar's direction.

"Patrice!" Abby spat. "Are you kidding me?"

"Oh, shut up!" Patrice spat back at her. "I'm not trying to die tonight, Abby. You go right ahead if you want to."

Patrice balled up the few hundred dollars and tossed them to Lamar's feet. "Much obliged," he said. "Now you're gonna get in that car and be gone. And I don't forget a face, I promise you that."

Abby and Patrice stood still for a moment, and then looked at each other with fear and rage in their eyes. Then they turned back towards their Uber, got in, and rode back out onto Tropicana Avenue, out towards the American Dream.

Chapter Nine

"**H**EY GUYS," KENDRA SAID INTO THE PHONE, "JUST wanted to let you know we're heading back this morning instead of a few days from now. We just sort of got bored at the house—one can only swim in an infinity pool for so many hours, you know? Anyway, we'll be back tonight. See you soon!"

She hung up, grateful she could just leave a voice-mail rather than have to recite her whole script directly to her parents.

"Nice detail about the infinity pool," Mitch said. He tapped the steering wheel with his fingers, obviously excited to finally be on the road again.

"Thanks," Kendra said, smiling. She looked out the passenger side window as the Strip passed by once again, rapidly falling away as the Mustang picked up speed and bent back around the big curve on the interstate, throttling back into the dusty purple expanse of the desert. "Think you'll ever come back out here?"

"Ugh," Mitch sighed. "Not anytime soon. You?"

"Part of me feels like we hardly scratched the surface here, that we didn't really get the experience," Kendra said. "But the other part of me feels like we got the *exact* Vegas experience. We were manipulated, robbed blind, and barely made it out alive."

Mitch sighed. "Yeah, I don't think we missed out on much. I wonder where Thelma and Louise are by now."

– – –

A few hours later, the landscape along the interstate started looking very familiar—to Kendra, at least. You never forget the place where you first fall in love.

"Dude, this is it," she said, tapping Mitch on the shoulder. "Exit ten. How does my breath smell?" she asked frantically, blowing a mouthful of hot air into Mitch's face.

"Mm," Mitch said, wincing. "Delightful."

Kendra fixed the straps of her slimming black tank top and push-up bra and finger-combed her hair. "Ugh, I look so basic. But it's all for him, right?"

"You're a vision," Mitch said, pulling off the highway and angling for Lauren's Roadside BBQ Pit's parking lot.

When she opened the door to the restaurant, Kendra searched the expanse of the dining room for Laurence like a lion surveys the dusty plain for an antelope. There he was, talking to a large family in a corner booth. Kendra took off across the restaurant, blowing past the hostess stand. The teenager working there frantically asked where she was going, but Kendra refused to turn back.

Kendra dove into the booth next to Laurence's current table. She not-so-subtly craned her neck above the divider between the booths, rapping her fingers on the greasy tabletop. Mitch sat across from her, with his back to Laurence. "You look like you're having an aneurysm," he said. "Cool it."

But Kendra's manic head-craning worked, and after taking the final order from the other table, Laurence turned to face Kendra. Time seemed to stop entirely as Kendra waited for her beloved to recognize her. She hung on the twitch of every muscle in Laurence's face, trying to make a note of every synapse firing in his brain. *If he doesn't recognize me, I swear to God . . .*

But then Laurence flashed his movie-star smile and strolled to the table. "Back already, I see."

Kendra willed herself to be cool, to make a smoother impression than she had the last time. "You bet," she said. "Couldn't get enough."

Mitch fought off an outburst of laughter. Instead, he tried to keep a normal human conversation going. "How have you been, Laurence?"

He waved the question off abashedly. "Oh, you

know me," he said. "Boring, boring, boring. Ribs, steak, steak, ribs . . . "

"You are *so* not boring," Kendra said, as if she and Laurence were the only two people in the room.

"Oh, hey," Laurence said to Kendra, "that was cool how you wrote your number on your check. I didn't think anybody did that anymore. Very 1950s."

Kendra's heart skipped a beat. "And do you . . . like the 1950s?"

Laurence guffawed. "Well sure! Simpler time, y'know? Nothing complicated like how we are now."

"Yeah," Kendra sighed. "I feel you. It was a time when two people could just . . . be together. There was a connection, they just got married and bought a house before they could think twice. I've always liked the sound of that."

Mitch couldn't resist. "Everyone was also horribly depressed and most wives felt trapped in the home by convention, unable to do what they wanted with their lives. Oh, and most marriages were a sham anyway."

Kendra shot him a death glare across the table.

A thick silence hung in the air, broken only when Laurence chirped, "So! Know what you'd like to eat?"

Kendra willed herself to look away from Mitch and put on a happy face. "How about a salad? You wrecked me last time." She let that settle for a second, before clarifying. "With that sandwich. You wrecked me with that sandwich."

Mitch briefly considered getting up from the table and running away. "I'll have a salad as well," he said.

"Sure thing," Laurence said. "We only have one salad though, I have to tell you."

"What is it?" both Kendra and Mitch asked simultaneously.

"Iceberg lettuce, bacon, steak strips, cherry tomatoes, and our house-made bleu cheese and bacon dressing," Laurence said, smiling. "And we're out of tomatoes."

Kendra beamed. "Sounds perfect."

Laurence gave them one final smile and walked away. As soon as he was gone, Kendra glared at Mitch.

"What are you doing, man?! What *was* that? About the 1950s?"

"I was just getting on your case," Mitch said. "Relax. Trying to have a little fun here. I mean, honestly, Kendra. What are you expecting to happen?"

"I don't know," Kendra sighed. "In my heart of hearts, I want Laurence to come back offering me his dead mom's wedding ring, but I know that's pretty unlikely."

"Just slightly," Mitch said.

Kendra put her head facedown on the table. "I know. But even if I could just get a wink, or a lingering touch on my hand, or *something.* This place isn't too far from home, you know. I can come back once a week!"

Mitch smiled. "I'm rooting for you, honestly. I'd love to regain some hope in the other men in this world. Both of us have been rejected, led on, *and* robbed at knifepoint. In the last two weeks."

An hour later, Kendra and Mitch walked out of the restaurant and back towards the parking lot. Kendra clutched a sacred piece of paper in her hand like a running back hurtling towards the end zone. She remained completely quiet until she climbed in the driver's side door of the Mustang. It was only then when she thrust her hands straight up victoriously, smacking the ceiling of the car.

"God, can you believe it?!" she exclaimed. Mitch giggled uncontrollably. "Look at those ten beautiful digits!" she shouted, pointing at the receipt where Laurence had scrawled his phone number.

"Those are some good digits," Mitch said.

"They're perfect. Perfect numbers. Literally perfect." Kendra kissed the receipt chastely, like she was at the altar with it.

"You have to wait at least a day until you text him," Mitch said. "Seriously. Any sooner and you're a stalker."

"Really?" Kendra said, pouting like a wounded puppy dog. "What about half a day? And I'll just be like, 'What's cookin'?' or something like that. It's a restaurant pun too! He'll love it. Right?"

"Okay, first of all, you can never say 'what's cookin','" Mitch said. "And secondly, no, you have to wait at least a day. Promise me."

Kendra groaned, but she was far from unhappy. "When he and I write the history of our beautiful unlikely love story," Kendra said, "it'll all start with one little text. One little innocent text. The cutest text anyone's ever sent to anyone: 'what's cookin'.' You'll see, Mitch. I'm gonna write a *book*."

With that, Kendra turned the key in the ignition and put down the top of the Mustang. It was time to ride home in style.

– – –

The sun was just setting behind the mountains in the west as the Mustang pulled into Kendra's driveway. Kendra put the car in park, and she and Mitch sat there as a certain song finished its course on the stereo: "*Mmm-bop, dip-a-dop, da-ooh* . . . "

"We made it," Kendra sighed, leaning back in the driver's seat. "I can't believe it."

Mitch rubbed his road-weary eyes. "If you hadn't thought so quickly and called Lamar, we might still be out there. Without a car, and without parents. Because they would have definitely disowned us forever."

Kendra didn't respond. She realized she had one more thing to bring up with Mitch. "Oh, hey, I have to tell you something," she said.

Mitch picked up on her dark tone. "What is it?" he asked worriedly.

"Remember when you found me sleeping at that gas station? I had this crazy dream while I was out there. But it was more than a dream. It felt like a vision or something."

Mitch raised an eyebrow and smirked, thinking this was the setup for a classic Kendra joke. "Oh, yeah?"

"No, seriously," she said. "I don't know if it was the heat, or the stress, or what, but . . . you know Jack the Jackal, the cartoon?"

"Yeah?"

"He like . . . appeared. In front of me. And he talked to me." Kendra squeezed her eyes shut. She couldn't bear seeing Mitch's expression while he tried to decide if his friend had completely lost her mind. "I know," she said, "it's totally weird."

"What'd he say?" Mitch asked.

"A bunch of cryptic stuff," Kendra said. "He kept saying that I missed watching cartoons and I was kidding myself if I said I wasn't that person anymore. Stuff like that."

"But you love Jack the Jackal!" Mitch said. "You have the doll!"

"That's what I said! But he kept saying that wasn't it, that I missed everything about that old routine. Getting up early, eating sugary cereal, all that stuff." Kendra sat back and rubbed her temples. "It was too weird and crazy to tell you about, at the time. But the more I think about it, I think it was my subconscious trying to tell me something. We set out on this trip because we wanted to act like adults. We wanted to cut loose and do our own thing, because for the first time, nobody could stop us."

"Right."

"And we did," Kendra said. "We definitely cut loose. And it was crazy . . . but not in a great way. I'm not sure we're Las Vegas people, Mitch."

Mitch rubbed his chin contemplatively. "Yeah," he said. "At least not the kind of Las Vegas people we were trying to be."

"I *do* kind of miss cartoons," Kendra admitted.

"And I miss all my old Audrey Hepburn movies," said Mitch. "Who says we can't still be those people?"

"Well, a lot of people say that," Kendra said, "but they're wrong. High school sucked, and this stupid song will definitely haunt me forever."

"Ugh," Mitch said, "me too."

"But now we get to go to the U in September, and we get a clean slate. We get to be ourselves again." Kendra smiled. She turned off the ignition, cutting off the Hanson brothers for the final time. "Want to watch some cartoons?"